NEUTRAL ZONE TRAP

THE DARTMOUTH COBRAS ~ AN OFF ICE NOVEL

BIANCA SOMMERLAND

Cover art by I'm No Angel Designs

NEUTRAL ZONE TRAP
The Dartmouth Cobras
Off Ice Novel
By
Bianca Sommerland

Cover art by I'm No Angel Designs

ALSO BY BIANCA SOMMERLAND

Sign up for my Newsletter for monthly prizes and teasers

The Dartmouth Cobras

Blind Pass

Butterfly Style

Cocky Shot

Game Misconduct

Defensive Zone

Breakaway

Offside

Delayed Penalty

Iron Cross

Goal Line

Line Brawl

Also

Deadly Captive

Collateral Damage

The End

Celestial Pets: Evil's Embrace

Solid Education

Street Smarts

Forbidden Steps

Rosemary Entwined

The Trip

Untamed (Feral Bonds)

Upper Class

Winter's Wrath Series

Backlash

Diminished

Inversion

Off Beat

Polished (New Rules Trilogy Book1)

Gilded (New Rules Trilogy Book 2)

CHAPTER 1

A dark street, an Uber driver who didn't say a word, and Braxton Richards reached the destination he'd been obsessing over for weeks. He stepped onto the sidewalk, avoiding curious glances from the guys standing on the edge of the sidewalk, smoking and laughing. They looked exactly how he'd expected them to look. Dressed either in all leather, or sparkly, colorful clothes.

Very gay.

Something he hadn't realized he needed. Seeing them shamelessly expressing themselves, being so relaxed about it, released some of the pressure that had been building in his chest for months. Pressure that increased every time he hung out with one of the other young players from the Dartmouth Cobras. His teammates were awesome, and people seemed accepting, but…

But of other people being gay, or bisexual, or in different kinds of relationships. There was this underlying current of how much harder it made life. How much harder it would make his life. His closest friend on the team, Dave Hunt, constantly repeated all the advice his dad, who was also his manager, gave him. The man was a jerk—not that he'd ever tell Hunt that—and blatantly homophobic, but it was hard not to admit he'd given Hunt some good advice.

They were too new to get away with the shit that was even rumored about the more experienced players. If they wanted to get anywhere as professional hockey players, they had to prove they weren't risky investments. That they'd appeal to long-time fans of the game. Fans like Hunt's father.

Which meant being serious about training. Impressive on the ice.

And good with the ladies. Talk of a young player dating hot models was a good boost for his career, which was why some managers made sure to set their clients up with several. There had to be a careful balance, there couldn't be talk of anything negative in the 'relationships', but a young man having all the fun the fans wished they could be having?

All good things.

So Braxton made sure he was seen with a few girls. Got drunk and let Hunt talk him into a threesome. His first time having sex. And it had been…

Weird. The girl was gorgeous. Sweet. The three of them had been talking and dancing all night before they went back to the hotel. But she didn't make Braxton hard. Hunt did.

Not by touching him or anything. As far as he knew, Hunt was straight. But the sounds of pleasure Hunt made when the girl…Cindy, her name had been Cindy. When Cindy pulled out Hunt's dick and started sliding her soft lips over it?

Yeah, that had been hot. Richards wished it had been his lips, but instead he'd fucked Cindy at Hunt's urging. The slick pressure hadn't done much for him at first. Hunt's whispers though? Hell, he couldn't get that out of his head for the longest time.

"Oh fuck, how does she feel, Richards?" Hunt let out a low moan that shot pleasure straight down the length of Braxton's dick. "Tell me."

Braxton eased back, then thrust in, loving the way Hunt panted as Cindy sucked him harder every time she was driven closer to the edge. All sloppy and out of control. Just like Braxton would be. "So fucking hot, Hunt. So wet. Does it feel good?"

Hunt groaned. "Yeah...don't stop."

He hadn't stopped, but he didn't come until Hunt did. Almost bit through his tongue to keep from screaming Hunt's name.

And the next day Hunt had gone back to talking about his father's advice and what his father thought of the queer players on the team. His tone was frustrated, but also...resigned. As though that's just how it was. He'd mentioned that his father would ditch him if he wasn't straight—he totally was. Very straight. He said it like a mantra. Like something he was afraid people wouldn't believe.

And yet...Braxton believed him. He believed him because he couldn't say the same, so he usually said nothing. Just nodded and hoped Hunt didn't see right through him.

Which was one of the reasons he'd come here tonight. He couldn't keep messing around with chicks because Hunt thought it was good for their image. Couldn't keep thinking about how hot his best friend was. He'd eventually slip up and destroy their friendship.

No way would he do that just to get off. Still, he couldn't pretend all the time. It was driving him out of his mind.

So he found a gay club after a lot of searches and lurking on forums. A club that was out of the way, in the warehouse district. Far enough that hopefully he wouldn't see anyone he knew. Or, if he did, they'd be desperate to keep their secrets to and leave him one night to be himself. To be somewhere he didn't have to pretend.

The club looked like the pictures he'd seen online, a bit disappointing, unlike the men hanging around outside. Some of the clubs he'd scrolled past during his searches were on busy streets surrounded by other clubs and tons of people, lining up to get in. He'd love to go to a place like that, but this was better. A forum full of guys who loved the place talked about it being extravagant, but safe. There was a code of silence. What happened here, stayed here. Like Vegas contained in one big, ugly grey building on the edge of Halifax.

Absolutely perfect.

He shivered as a cool breeze picked up, pressing against his back as though to urge him on, or force him to turn around and go home. A home he shared with a veteran player who he'd barely exchanged more than a 'Do you need to use the bathroom?' before a shower.

Tonight was his night to explore and no way was he backing out now. He squared his shoulders, smoothing his hands over the light, dark blue wool jacket he was wearing, along with skin-tight dark red jeans and covering a black mesh shirt he wasn't sure had been the best choice for his first night like this alone. He could always keep his jacket on, or…

See how you feel once you get inside, Richards. He hesitated at another chorus of laughter from the small crowd on the sidewalk. Just get in there!

He forced himself to move, sparring the group a brief smile before heading inside. He felt their eyes on him as he let the heavy metal door slam shut behind him. Tried to keep his breaths slow and steady as a bouncer strode over to check his ID.

About twice his age, wearing a black T-shirt and black jeans, the large man handed back his ID and gave him a considering look. "First time?"

Inclining his head, Braxton met the man's eyes. "I've heard good things."

That made the man smile. "I'm not surprised. Check out the show, we've got a good line-up of dancers tonight. And my husband, Terry, is working the floor. He's the one with the pink and white hair. When you see him, tell him Gordon says hi and he'll look out for you."

"Really? That's cool." Braxton's cheeks heated. "Thank you."

"Hey, I was your age once. Coming here alone? That was brave of you." The man hesitated. "Anyone give you trouble and you let me know, all right? Or tell Terry. You want a good time and you'll find it, but nothing happens that you don't want, got it?"

Braxton swallowed hard. He hadn't expected to need that kind of warning. This felt like stepping on the ice when Dominik Mason, the team's enforcer, wasn't around. Which rarely happened, but he was always more careful, knowing the man wasn't watching his back. One wrong move and Braxton would be crushed.

"Hey, I didn't say that to scare you. I'm serious, Terry knows the crowd. He won't let anything bad happen." Gordon patted Braxton's shoulder. "Have fun. And tip well."

"I will. Thanks again." Braxton took a deep breath and continued inside.

The place was crowded to the point that it was hard to get anywhere, smelling of sweat and candy and strong alcohol. He inched his way forward, lips parting as he spotted a dancer up on a small round platform, surrounded by men and women, dancing seductively to the heavy beat of the deafening music. He wanted to keep watching, but the crowd was pushing at him. He couldn't breathe with so many people so close. The flashing neon lights sweeping over the club were making him dizzy.

Ducking his head, he pressed forward until he came to the edge of the table circling the stage. There were less people standing here, more seated either around the tables or on the stools by the stage. There were no empty tables, but the two empty stools in front of him looked promising. He grabbed one and sat to gain his bearings.

The music quieted and all focus turned to the stage. He started to look over too, but someone stopped at his side and he jumped.

Grinning at him, the man with light brown skin, warm brown eyes, and pink and white hair leaned close. "The show's about to start. Can I get you anything before it does? I don't usually pass by here again until it's over so I don't block anyone's view."

"A beer would be great."

"Any preference?"

"Not really, they all taste the same." He wrinkled his nose. "Just the easiest thing." He recalled Gordon's suggestion. "Oh, and Gordon told me he says 'Hi'."

Terry laughed. "That's my man. You're adorable and he's a worrier. How about I get you something tastier than beer? Do you like sweet? Sour? Salty?"

Brow furrowed, Braxton shrugged. "I'm not fussy. Sour stuff I love though."

"Perfect! I'll be right back."

As Terry disappeared into the crowd, Braxton turned back to the stage, folding his arms across his chest and trying not to notice the odd glances from the men, and the few women and other people around him. He felt like he was the one on the stage, with the spotlight on him, his inexperience stamped in the middle of his for all to see. Which was silly, people had to be doing their own thing?

But those people had been here before.

And he couldn't be more out of place if he tried.

"It would help if you took off your jacket." A man settled in the stool beside him, setting his glass on the thin ledge before the stage. "You're drawing attention because you look ready to run."

The man's voice sent a delicious shiver down Braxton's spine, deep and low, with the soothing quality of the ocean at night lapping the shore, the rumble of thunder in the distance as a storm approached. He had to count to five in his head to regain his composure before he looked at the man.

Then he forgot to breathe at all. The man's voice was soothing, but the man himself was everything but. Dark brown hair just long enough to look soft, but short enough not to distract from his chiseled features. Dark eyes with a golden touch and a hint of green. Smooth, tanned skin, a hint of stubble on his sharp jaw, and thick muscles under a dark green Henley shirt that was meant to show off every sculpted one. The man was a little too rough around the edges to be traditionally handsome, but he was alluring, with a strong presence, the look of a soldier, or what Braxton imagined one would look like—and did in every one of his fantasies.

A hint of amusement in the man's eyes brought Braxton back to his words. His jacket. Yeah...he should probably take it off. But he couldn't.

He cleared his throat. "I had an idea of how people would dress here, and got something I liked, but I feel weird now. My jacket is...neutral."

"Now I'm curious." The man's laugh was absolutely devastating. Like a soft caress slipping down Braxton's spine. "But whatever you're most comfortable with. I just thought I'd let you know the jacket is a dead giveaway that you're fresh meat."

Braxton wrinkled his nose. "Is that why you're talking to me?"

"That, and I've been where you are. Not as young either." The man folded his arms on the ledge, close to his drink. "My work took all my focus, and I liked it that way. I didn't want to consider anything that would distract me. I achieved everything I wanted in my career and then decided Grindr hookups weren't enough for me. I wanted to socialize a bit." He made a vague gesture at the club around them. "So I started coming here."

"I considered Grindr, but the idea of meeting some random stranger?" Braxton shuddered. "Can't do it."

The man nodded slowly. "So you're looking for a relationship?"

Am I? He didn't even know. For now, just talking to someone was good. Someone like him who wouldn't tell him how bad hooking up with a man would be for his career. Who didn't care about his career. Who saw…the real him.

"I'm looking for…this." He shrugged as the music started building up again, and smoke filled the stage. "Being somewhere I don't have to hide who I really am. I can't do that with my job. With my friends. It's…stressful."

"I get that. Believe me." The man sat back as Terry returned with Braxton's drink. His expression hardened as Terry leaned close, whispering something in his ear. He glanced over at Braxton. "Am I bothering you?"

Terry looked at him too and Braxton shrank in his stool, staring at the yellow tinged drink that had been set in front of him. The man was nice, and Braxton was enjoying their conversation. But maybe Terry was worried for a reason.

Yeah, because you're new here and he doesn't think you can make your own decisions.

Could he though? This was…different. Picking up a chick with Hunt was easy. Being a pro athlete? Yeah, there were girls really into that. But Braxton didn't want them.

And now he was on the other side. The one being picked up. Maybe.

He wanted to see where this went.

He met Terry's concerned gaze. "He's not bothering me, but thank you."

"All right, honey." Terry placed his hand on Braxton's shoulder and leaned close. "He's a good man, I'm not afraid he'll do anything bad. But...baby, don't expect too much. Some people are only their real selves here, you feel me?"

"I do." Braxton licked his bottom lip. "I think...I think that's me too."

"I hate hearing that." Terry patted his cheek. "But I hope you'll come back. No matter what, okay? You're welcome here."

With that, Terry slipped away, serving the rest of the drinks on his tray around as the show began.

A quick sip of the drink in front of him and Braxton let out a soft, pleased sound of appreciation. He'd mostly drank beer and a few shots of tequila, but this was so much better. Like sour lemon drops with a kick. He took another sip and licked his lips.

"You should try this." He turned to the man at his side, holding up the drink. "It's so much better than beer."

The man chuckled. "I've had a whiskey sour before, but you're making me wonder if I'm missing something, never having it here." He took the glass and tipped it to his lips. "Oh yeah, that's very good."

"Do you want one? I can ask him to get another if you—"

"Tell me something..." The man paused. Waited, brow arched.

"Richards. Or...well, my name's Braxton." Head flooded his cheeks.

Very smooth.

Inclining his head, the man handed back his glass. "Ryan Hamilton."

"Nice to meet you." Braxton took a long gulp. He couldn't tear his attention from the man, even though whatever was happening on stage was drawing the attention of everyone else in the room. He recalled what Ryan had said when he'd first come over and started undoing his jacket. "And you're right, I shouldn't be wearing this in here, I—"

"Wait." Ryan's eyes heated as he took in the mesh shirt in the part of the jacket. "Fuck, you take that off and you're going to have tons of offers. You're so fucking new and it's too fucking obvious. Keep it on."

Braxton stilled. Chewed on his bottom lip. "I'm not that young. And maybe I want people to offer. Tomorrow I have to go back to my life and pretend I'm...someone else."

"That's tomorrow." Ryan reached out and wrapped his hand around Braxton's wrist. "Tonight you can forget about all that. I won't let anyone near you."

Laughing, Braxton stared at Ryan's hand. "Kinda defeats the purpose."

"Not if you let me take you home with me." Ryan's jaw tightened, as though he regretted making the offer. He released Braxton and shifted back. "I shouldn't have said that. You're here to have fun. Why don't you watch the dancers and—"

There was no way he could even look at the dancers now. A man like Ryan hitting on him was beyond anything he'd hoped for tonight. He wanted Ryan's hand on his again. Wanted him to keep looking at him like he was fucking edible. Wanted him to satisfy every urge that had been denied over and over again.

"What happens if I go home with you?" Braxton wasn't usually this bold. When sex was involved, Hunt was there, leading the way and making sure they checked off all the right boxes. Find a woman who looked right if pictures leaked. Was famous enough to not want to talk badly about them for attention. Was willing and knew exactly what to expect from them.

Which was a good time.

But Braxton wasn't trying to erase that woman. He was trying to erase Hunt. Which would be harder. Hunt was his friend. Was close to him. He could talk to Hunt.

About everything except something like this. But so far, Ryan seemed to get it. How new this was. How important. Maybe

Ryan was exactly who Braxton needed. Not just a hookup, but someone willing to explore all these feelings.

"Braxton, I'm not looking for a relationship. If you are..." Ryan shook his head. "Don't. Not yet. You've got time for that. But you need to be careful. A lot of men here will leave you feeling used and not care that you enjoy yourself. I'll make sure you do."

"I'm not sure what I'm looking for."

Ryan's lips curved. He leaned in close and whispered in Braxton's ear. "If you come with me, I'll let you suck my dick, then I'll fuck you so you know how you like it. You'll be hard to please after I'm done with you, but that's a good thing. You deserve someone willing to leave you begging for more."

"*Fuck...*"

"Yeah...imagine that. Tell me I can touch you. I want to give you a taste of what I want to do to you." Ryan's lips brushed his throat. He licked Braxton's neck when he nodded, reaching down and placing a hand on his knee. "You've been playing a part and it's left you so fucking needy." His hand moved up Braxton's thigh, making his dick swell. "I won't be done with you after fucking you once. I'll give you a bit of time to recover, then I'll take you again. And again. You'll wake up in the morning too sore for me to do more than tell you how fucking hard you made me come. And maybe then I'll get you off one last time before I let you go, because I'm mean that way."

"I want that." And he did. Holy fuck, he wasn't sure he'd ever wanted anything more. "I'm scared to ask what you'd do to me if you were being nice."

Ryan's tongue flicked over Braxton's ear. "If I was being nice, I'd walk away now. But I won't. Because what fun would that be? You're already mine."

He really was. He couldn't think of anything but Ryan's words. His every nerve was fixated on Ryan's touch. All he cared about was finding the strength to stand so he could follow Ryan out of there.

From the corner of his eye, he spotted Terry, arms folded over his chest, shaking his head. The man didn't think he could make his own decisions. He thought he needed to protect Braxton. Just like everyone on the team.

Just like Hunt.

But they were smothering him. And he wanted this.

Even if only for tonight.

I can have tonight, right?

Slipping out of his stool, he met Ryan's level gaze.

"Let's go."

CHAPTER 2

What the hell are you thinking, Hamilton?

After finishing his drink, Ryan Hamilton nodded to the young man at his side and started toward the exit, schooling his features to hide the doubt echoing in his skull. This wasn't how he'd planned the night to go. He usually sought out experienced partners, sometimes even men he'd enjoyed a night with before, men whose only interest was a good time. Men like him.

Braxton was a wildcard, one Ryan usually wouldn't play with, but he couldn't ignore the draw of him when he'd seen him walk across the club. Eyes wide, both eager and a little afraid, seeming shy one moment, then bold the next.

Ryan wasn't the only one who'd noticed the boy, which was what got him moving. Before he'd reached the seating around the stage he'd been cut off by a man he'd fooled around with once, Michel Schauer. Half blocking Ryan's path, Michel turned to face him, a smirk on his lips.

"You can't be serious. You want him?" Michel laughed and leaned close to Ryan, speaking low, but loud enough to be heard over the

music. "I thought you weren't looking for a pet? Just a toy to play with for the night now and then. That was your excuse the last time I offered, anyway."

Ryan's jaw tensed as he looked over the slender man with the spiky platinum hair and big brown eyes. Extremely attractive, but him being sexy didn't erase the fact that he was a toxic bastard.

Michel claimed to be a submissive—they'd met at a different club and done a fairly light scene. But the man was selfish and manipulative. He spoke down to those he considered beneath him, pulled attitude with anyone in authority, then turned on the charm in the blink of an eye to get his own way.

By the end of the night Ryan's skin crawled just being near Michel, but he'd finished the scene—an intense flogging since Michel was a regular at the club and had a few Doms he'd scened with in the past as reference—and provided aftercare. He'd wanted to end things there, but Michel somehow guilted him into taking him home.

They'd had lackluster sex and then Michel left. But not before shooting Ryan the same smirk he wore now. One that said he knew who was really in control.

The only reason Ryan had even fucked the man was because he couldn't quite put his finger on why the asshole made him so uncomfortable until much later, when he'd pieced together the little things. The way Michel spoke. The way he looked at people. The way other submissives avoided him. There were whispers that he didn't respect the club's rules of consent, but no one ever came forward. It was still enough to get him banned from that club, but there must not have been any complaints here.

Yet.

Ryan would give Terry a heads up when he had a chance. This was the first time he'd seen Michel skulking around the joint. And it would damn well be the last.

No way was he letting him anywhere near the young man who'd caught both their eyes.

He gave Michel a cold look. "Don't test me."

"Test you? Whatever do you mean?" Michel let out a light laugh. "This could be fun. Let's see which of us he'll choose." His lips curved. "Unless you'd like to share?"

"Like fuck." All right, Ryan was done playing nice. He stepped forward, forcing Michel back. "You have two choices. You leave now, or I'll ask Terry if I can do him the favor of escorting you out."

With a little pout, Michel made a dismissive gesture and turned away. "No need to be so dramatic. This place is boring anyway. Everyone's so uptight."

"Be careful, Michel." Ryan's eyes narrowed when Michel snorted, inching his way through the tight crowd toward the door. "Next time I see you, it might be in a more official capacity."

At that, Michel turned, feigned shock on his face. "I hope not, Detective. But if it pleases you, sir, I shall be on my best behavior."

Not good enough, but unless someone felt safe filing a report, there was nothing else Ryan could do. He would be asking around though. His job was to protect people from predators like Michel.

For tonight, he'd protected one.

Which should have been the end of it. He'd observed Braxton for a bit, realized Terry was in momma-bear mode, and considered looking elsewhere for the night's entertainment. That would've been smarter.

Instead he convinced himself it wouldn't hurt to talk to the young man. Sat close to him and took in his hesitant smiles, the way he moved, the longing and hunger in his eyes as he was far too honest about why he'd come.

Then he showed Ryan that damn mesh shirt. Fuck him, he wasn't good at resisting temptation and that was exactly what Braxton was. Every sleek, tightly muscled, wiry inch of him begged for Ryan's touch. Ryan battled with the protective urges in his head and gave in to the lust overpowering it.

No matter what, Braxton would be going home with someone tonight. He was practically vibrating with need. Need that Ryan could satisfy.

Tonight.

Only tonight. He couldn't offer more. But he could make sure Braxton was safe. And give him an experience he'd never forget.

Once they reached his car, Ryan glanced over at Braxton, frowning as the young man reached for the door handle. Without knowing more than his name, Braxton was ready to just drive off with him. Which, with the wrong person, could end up with him being another cold case sitting on Ryan's desk.

"Take a picture of my license plate and send it to a friend." Ryan held Braxton's gaze when the man blinked at him. "You don't know me. There's the possibility that I rented the car under a fake name, but at least it's some way to track me—or anyone else you're leaving a public setting with—if you go missing."

Braxton's cheeks flushed. He folded his arms over his chest. "Should I be worried? You sound like a cop."

"I am one." Amusement slanted Ryan's lips when Braxton stared at him. "Unless you used a fake ID to get into the club, you have nothing to worry about."

"I didn't." Braxton hiked up his chin, all defensive now. "Do you want to double check while I get that picture of your license plate? Make sure this is all legit and everything?"

"No need. Gordon's good at spotting fakes." He looked over Braxton thoughtfully. "I don't put you much past twenty, though."

"I'm nineteen." Braxton hugged himself a little tighter. "Too young?"

"Yes and no. But like I told you earlier, I was your age once.

And lucky enough to get with a few older men who treated me well." Which was the only reason Ryan didn't immediately tell Braxton to go home and find someone his own age. For a relationship that would be best. But for what they'd do tonight?

Braxton knew what he wanted. And Ryan had no problem giving it to him.

His response seemed to relax Braxton. After letting out a heavy sigh at Ryan's pointed look, he went and took a picture of the license plate. Sent a text. Then returned to the front passenger-side door. "Did they pick you up at a club and tell you how good they were going to fuck you?"

Ryan grinned, enjoying how straightforward the young man was being, now that they'd gotten the important matters out of the way. "Yes. And they weren't lying. You'll benefit from what they taught me tonight."

Inhaling roughly, Braxton lowered his gaze. "I…I want that. But I'm not sure I'm…any good."

Exactly how Ryan had felt his first time. But he'd been too nervous to confess as much to his lover. He'd simply let things happen and was lucky the man he'd been with was patient. A quality Ryan himself had honed over years as both a Dom and an officer. He'd let the young man go at his own pace—with some encouragement as they both figured out what that was. So far, Braxton seemed to enjoy being told what would come next, which suited Ryan just fine. He'd take his cues from how Braxton reacted to his words, building up the man's confidence by showing him that his inexperience didn't make him any less desirable.

Making his way around the car, Ryan moved close to Braxton, tugging his arms apart and bringing them up around the back of his neck. Sliding his hands down Braxton's sides, he brought his lips close to Braxton's, speaking softly. "You'll be good because you'll let me take what I want from you." He brushed his tongue over Braxton's bottom lip. "You'll do exactly as I say when I have you on your knees. When I strip you down and lay you in my bed. When I have you under me, begging."

"Fuck... Yes. I can do that."

"I know you can." He pressed against Braxton, letting him feel his dick swelling in his black jeans. Enjoying the pressure of Braxton's length, already fully hard and straining toward his own. "If you change your mind, at any point, tell me. But I don't think you will."

Tipping his chin up, Braxton caught Ryan's bottom lip between his teeth. Sucked lightly, making all the blood surge down until his dick pulsed, wanting those lips around it now. Braxton let out a soft groan. "I won't. But I'm not sure I can wait until we get to wherever you're taking me."

At that, Ryan chuckled. He eased back, then cupped Braxton's cheek. "I'm taking you to my house. And you'll be a good boy and wait."

Braxton slumped back against the car as Ryan moved away from him. "You're not even gonna kiss me first?"

Ryan shook his head. "Not until you're naked. I don't want you to forget what this is. One amazing night."

Brow furrowed, Braxton looked down again. "If things are amazing, why wouldn't you want more?"

A great big sign that Ryan should end this now. Bring Braxton back into the club. Help him find someone who'd consider a date after. Maybe a relationship. He didn't think the man needed that yet, but what did he know?

"I can't give you more, Braxton. We're staying right here if you don't understand that."

There. He couldn't get much clearer.

But he wouldn't lie and say he wasn't relieved when Braxton nodded.

"I get it."

"Good." He pulled out his key and unlocked the door. "Then get in."

A one-night-stand. Totally fine. And honestly, Braxton *did* get it. Ryan thought he was hot and that was fucking amazing. The man pushed every button Braxton hadn't known he had. He couldn't imagine one night being enough, but that's how things like this went, right?

Fast and wild and erotic and then...done.

But this was so damn new and he couldn't ignore the fact that he couldn't have gone home with just anyone. He'd thought it wouldn't be an issue, but if a guy hadn't talked to him? Hadn't made him feel comfortable?

He'd have stayed at the club.

With Ryan, leaving had been easy. Sitting beside him in the car, looking out the window because the alternative was staring and making things weird, Braxton considered how fast he'd gone from being completely lost and overwhelmed to being…here. With a man who was everything he'd ever dreamed of.

Could someone get sexier the longer you looked at them? Because when he'd first seen Ryan, he'd thought he was kinda hot. Then he spoke and he was irresistible. Then he'd gotten all take charge and there was no word for how much Braxton craved whatever he could have from the man.

One night. One hour. Hell, one damn minute and there was something inside him that had been so empty, now filled up to overflowing. Maybe that was all this was. Finally, someone letting him be himself. Accepting him as though who he was wasn't the end of the world. It was natural…even desirable.

There were guys on the team who'd probably have given Braxton that feeling, but part of him still needed to keep this side of himself separate. He saw what happened when identity overruled talent. How people acted different.

Someone like Shawn Pischlar, or Zachary Pearce, could get through it. They were established. Had fans and solid contracts and a future in the league. Braxton was still a nobody. Lucky to even be in the lineup every night. Easy to leave out if he messed up.

He loved his career. Loved playing hockey. And as hard as it was to hide part of himself, he'd do it. At least until he proved he was worth keeping.

They slowed in front of a small house near the edge of Dartmouth, on a long road near Bell Lake, an area he hadn't been around much, but he recognized some of the landmarks from passing through on the way to visit other players for dinners and get-togethers. When Ryan pulled into the driveway, Braxton sat up and undid his seatbelt. Took a deep breath. And did his best to lay out the next play as though he was on the ice and had little time to make an impact.

If all he had with Ryan was tonight, he hoped he wouldn't be easy to forget.

Because I already know Ryan won't be.

After parking the car, Ryan got out and headed straight for the front door, tension in his every step as he surveyed the area. He stopped in front of the door, waited for Braxton to join him, then unlocked the door. Stepped aside to let Braxton pass, followed, then locked the door and a deadbolt behind him.

His lips slanted at Braxton's questioning look. "I arrested the leader of a biker gang recently and came home to a few…interesting packages. We found the culprit, so no need to worry, but I tend to be vigilant. Just in case."

"That's smart."

"I like to think so." Ryan caught Braxton's wrist and pulled him close, laughing against Braxton's lips when he gasped.

"Unless you ask me not to, I'm going to take these clothes off you. You teased me showing me that shirt. Such a bad boy."

Braxton shivered, Ryan calling him a 'bad boy' sending a sweet chill up his spine. He couldn't find his voice, but after holding his gaze for a brief moment, Ryan seemed to get the answer he wanted. He shoved Braxton's jacket off his shoulders, letting it fall to the floor even as he tugged up the mesh shirt that covered next to nothing.

"Mmm." Braxton tipped his head back against the door as Ryan's lips trailed the length of his throat. He pressed his eyes shut as Ryan undid his skin-tight jeans, his blood pulsing into his cock as a firm, rough hand wrapped around it. "Oh fuck, that. Keep doing that."

"Take your pants off. Let me look at you." Ryan gave him a few lazy strokes, then stepped back, waiting.

Kicking off his shoes, Braxton shoved at his jeans until they were low enough to kick off as well. He ditched his socks, goosebumps rising all over his skin as Ryan's hot gaze took in every inch of him.

"I'd take you for a dancer, but these muscles are too thick. Especially your legs." Ryan moved in, brushing his hand up Braxton's thigh, his other hand curving under his jaw. "You're fucking gorgeous, you know that?"

Fighting to control his breathing, Braxton shrugged. "People like looking at me, but I have these muscles because I need them on the ice."

"On the..." Ryan's brow furrowed. "Jesus, please tell me you're not a hockey player."

Dick out, completely naked, that was the last thing Braxton wanted to hear. That hesitation. As though the wrong answer might end things.

"I am, but the way I see it, that doesn't matter. I don't see a badge when I look at you. I see the man who promised to fuck me." He'd never cared about being naked in front of a chick, but being naked now had him completely vulnerable. Part of his mind always reminded him he should want the woman. That he should make things good for her. And he did. But tonight wasn't about that. And he hoped Ryan couldn't look at him and just walk away. "Promised to ruin me for anyone else."

"Oh, I will. But I should've been worried about pictures. About what being seen with you could do to me."

"Are you?"

"Not right now I'm not." Ryan placed his hands on Braxton's shoulders. "Don't move. I need to taste you."

The pressure of Ryan's lips had Braxton closing his eyes and savoring the heat, the subtly sweet, heady taste of Ryan's mouth, the way his lips and tongue sparked a fierce desire he'd never known before. He'd had a crush on Hunt, but one kiss from Ryan and the other man was erased from his mind. Less than a memory.

All that remained was Ryan. The way he guided Braxton with the smooth dip of his tongue. His fingers digging into Braxton's hips as he drew him even closer, biting his bottom lip, gliding his hands up Braxton's back and into his hair, tugging until Braxton was melting against him, drinking in every sensation as though he couldn't exist anywhere but right here, right now.

His lips slipped across Braxton's cheek, brushing his ear. "Kneel for me. I've been wanting that hot mouth on my dick all night."

Braxton dropped to his knees, inhaling roughly as Ryan unzipped his jeans and pulled out his dick. Long and thick, dark reddish purple at the head, like he'd been holding back too long. He didn't wait before pressing against Braxton's lips, but he tugged Braxton's hair when he tried to press forward and take him in all the way.

"Slow down. There's no rush. Not yet." He stroked Braxton's

cheek. "Tip your head back. I'm going to fuck this sweet mouth until I'm so close I can't take any more. Then you'll get a little break. Show me how good you can be for me first."

Being good sounded perfect. Braxton wanted Ryan to enjoy him. That was most important. He tipped his head back, cursing under his breath when he jerked away on instinct as Ryan slid in too deep.

"You're doing good. Relax your throat. Swallow around me." Ryan cupped the back of his head. Pressed in. Deeper, even deeper, then stopped when Braxton gagged. "Swallow. Breathe in as I pull back, then let me in a little more. There." This time, Ryan drew back before Braxton's gag reflex kicked in. Thrust forward before it could recover. "Oh fuck, you have the hottest mouth. I could fuck your face over and over, just watching you look up at me like that." He let out a soft moan and tightened his grip on Braxton's hair. "A little more. Just take it. Yes, like that."

The steady stroke of Ryan's dick over his tongue, going in deeper every time, had desperate noises escaping as Braxton gasped in air. Precum wet the tip of his dick, cooling in the soft breeze coming from an open window somewhere.

Ryan's dick throbbed and he pulled away, gripping the base of his dick and holding still for a few beats before stroking the tip over Braxton's lips. "So good. I'd keep going, but you're ready to be fucked, aren't you? Unless you'd rather I come now and torture you until I'm ready to go again."

That sounded like the best and worst thing and Braxton wasn't sure how to answer. Knowing he could give Ryan that kind of pleasure made his chest swell and chased away all his insecurity. He loved the taste of Ryan, but he wanted to feel him everywhere. He could have both…

He tugged his bottom lip between his teeth and gazed up at Ryan. "I need to know what you want from me."

Stroking his hair, Ryan nodded slowly. "I see that. Come." He held out his hand, taking hold of Braxton's wrist and drawing him to his feet. "I want you in my bed where I can take my time with this gorgeous body. You're testing my control and we can't have that."

Braxton grinned as Ryan tucked himself into his jeans without zipping them and led the way to his bedroom. Like the rest of the house the room was sparsely decorated, all natural colors, dark greens and rich browns, the furniture solid and efficient, wood and metal, meant to last. A hint of cologne lingered in the air, a deep, musky undertone with a warm aroma he couldn't quite define, but breathed in every time he was close to Ryan. A scent that reminded him of cool nights sitting close to a campfire, the ocean in the distance along with the leaves and the trees all combining to make every inhale part of an experience that stayed with him long after he'd returned to his real life. Just thinking of the scent could trigger a wonderful memory.

After tonight, he had a feeling the memory would change to include the man who drew him to his bed and eased him onto the soft, forest green comforter.

Laying over him, hands braced by his shoulders, Ryan smiled. "Much better. Are you comfortable?"

"Very." Braxton closed his eyes as Ryan's lips drifted down his neck, then to his collarbone where a flick of his tongue sent a shiver of pleasure along every nerve. He tried to hold still as Ryan continued down to his chest, but he needed more. His dick was painfully hard. Ryan taking his time was driving him insane. He bit back a smile, keeping his tone light. "I could take a nap right now. Your bed is awesome."

Lifting his head, Ryan gave him a dark look. "Ah, so you're a bit of a brat, are you? If I had more time I'd punish you for trying to rush me, but instead I'm going to make you decide what happens next."

"But…" All right, that was not what Braxton wanted. He'd thought teasing Ryan a bit would be fun. Instead, he'd gotten all the pressure back on him. And Ryan had stopped kissing him and was just…waiting. He groaned and shook his head. "I loved you fucking my mouth and seeing you so close to losing control. I want to know I can do that to you. That you want me so much you can't hold back."

Ryan's lips slanted. "I never lose control, Braxton. But if you think I don't want to fuck you right now, you're wrong. I simply want to make sure you're ready."

Swallowing hard, Braxton considered what would happen if he told Ryan he didn't need him to be so careful. If he told him he was ready.

He met Ryan's eyes. "I am."

Pushing away from him, Ryan reached over to slide open a drawer on his nightstand. He grabbed an open box of condoms and a bottle of lube, dropping them on the bed at Braxton's side. "Have you played with your ass before Braxton? Or let anyone else do it?"

Cheeks burning, Braxton shook his head. His pulse quickened as his dick gave another painful throb.

"A shame, I think you'd enjoy it."

"Aren't you going to—"

"Yes, impatient one. But if you're going to enjoy this, I have to prepare you." Ryan's tone was rough as he opened the lube and pressed Braxton's thighs apart with his own. "Look at that tight little hole. I can't wait to stretch you open around me. Let's see how much you can take."

Gaze fixed on Braxton's face, Ryan stroked one slick finger around his rim, smirking when Braxton tensed and hissed in a sharp breath. The sensation was like nothing he'd ever felt before. He couldn't decide if he wanted to jerk away or press forward.

He did neither. His whole body shook as he focused on Ryan, lips parting as Ryan's finger eased in.

"Oh fuck..." The slight burn didn't distract from the pleasure. If anything, intensified it. The need, the excitement, the desire to make sure Ryan enjoyed him in every way. "Should I move?"

The question seemed to please Ryan, because his eyes warmed. "No. Lift your arms above your head and clasp your hand to your wrist. You're mine right now, Braxton. I'll enjoy toying with you for a bit. I don't think it'll take much to get you begging."

At first, Braxton tried to obey, but as Ryan eased his finger in and out, keeping his hands in place got harder. As a second finger joined the first he reached down and grabbed Ryan's shoulders, lifting his hips to take him in deeper.

Ryan swiftly grabbed his hands, shoving them back and holding his wrist in a firm grip as he maintained the steady pace of his fingers penetrating Braxton's ass. He used the pressure of his body on Braxton's thighs to open him more, while holding him still.

"You were doing well, pressing against me and letting me in, but you're tightening up now. Relax and let me have you. You won't regret it."

Relaxing was almost impossible when he was this turned on, but Ryan's voice, the control in his tone, settled him into the rhythm of his deepening touch. Ryan rewarded him by adding more lube and pressing his fingers in all the way, curving them until he hit a spot that tore a cry from Braxton's throat.

The pleasure was deep and intense and not moving got even harder. His eyes teared as he fought the urge, gasping as Ryan focused on that one spot.

"*Pleasepleaseplease!*" Braxton wasn't even sure what he was begging for, only that he was going to come and he wanted more than Ryan's fingers inside him when he did. "Stop... Don't...Please..."

"Shh, just a little more. You're almost there."

Another finger. Braxton's whole body jerked. Precum spilled over the head of his dick. A rush of sensations gathered as his balls lifted and his muscles tensed.

Ryan circled the base of his dick, and beneath his balls, with his thumb and forefinger, making a tight ring that held back the release that had been so close. He'd let go of Braxton's wrists, but there was no way Braxton could move now. He was locked in the fierce grip of heightened arousal, nothing but Ryan's hold keeping him from falling apart.

"Deep breath. There you go. You're lucky I've decided to play nice." Ryan's tone took on a wicked edge as he languidly fucked Braxton with three fingers, still gripping his cock. "I'd love to teach you to hold back on your own. To wait for me to let you come. If I decided to at all."

That sounded painful. And scary. And amazing. Giving Ryan that kind of control over him? Fuck, he'd do anything to make that his new reality. To know he could have this and more, long after tonight.

Maybe...maybe he could. Maybe Ryan was saying that because his resolve was fading. If Braxton pleased him, this wouldn't be the end.

Rising up, Ryan drew out of Braxton and shoved down his jeans. He grabbed a condom, rolling it on, then slicking his dick with lube. "You should see how fucking hot your shiny little hole looks. Fuck..." He pressed the head of his dick against Braxton's ass. "Still so tight. Do you think you can take me, Braxton? Press back like you did before. Let me see that ass open for me." He lifted Braxton's knees, hooking them over his forearms as he eased in a bit more. "The next time I fuck you, it will be hard and fast. But now, I want you to feel every inch of me filling you up. Do you feel it, pet? How hard you make me?"

Braxton couldn't make his mouth form words. The stretching, the pressure, the heat of Ryan inside him stole the ability to do more than absorb each erotic sensation as his body adjusted. When Ryan stopped moving, Braxton gaped up at him, panting.

"Tell me, Braxton. I want to hear how much you like being my little slut for the night. How much you want me to use this tight ass."

Licking his lips, Braxton nodded. He wasn't sure how Ryan made 'slut' sound like such a good thing. Wasn't sure why his chest tightened when he'd called him 'pet'. But he wanted it all. And he knew he had to say something to get it.

"I want you to use it until I can't feel anything besides you. Until you've marked every part of me and I can't imagine being a slut for anyone else." He groaned as Ryan drew out, then pressed back in, stretching him more. "Oh God, your dick feels incredible. I need it. I need it all."

Ryan made a soft, please sound. "You'll have it, but I'm enjoying the view." He lifted Braxton's legs higher, to his shoulders, freeing his hands to curve under Braxton's ass, spreading his cheeks as he kept his gaze fixed on where his dick slid in further. "You're made for this. Fuck, I'm going to pound this ass so hard before I'm done with you."

"Don't be. I'm yours for as long as you want me."

"I know." Ryan drew out, added lube yet again, then let his dick glide in all the way. "Perfect. So fucking perfect."

The burn was gone, leaving behind nothing but a fullness and heat and pressure, driving Braxton higher and higher as though there was no limit and he'd simply be in this zone, wrapped up in lust and pleasure, forever. With Ryan moving into him, faster and faster, stroking his thighs and whispering encouraging words as he positioned Braxton almost bent in half so he could drive in even deeper.

Without warning, the sensations rolled over Braxton, bursting from the base of his spine as he came, shouting and shaking as spurts of cum hit his chest. He clenched and Ryan cursed, slamming in one last time and gripping Braxton's hips as his dick pulsed within.

He leaned heavily on Braxton's legs, letting out a rough laugh before letting his dick slip free from his ass. "No control, but I showed less than I usually do, so I can't complain. Next time I won't be so generous though." He removed the condom, put it in the foil package, and tossed it in the trash under the nightstand. "We'll see how long you can last."

With a sleepy smile, Braxton pulled himself up to rest his head on the pillows. "So you're not kicking me out yet?"

"No. I told you, we have one night." Ryan lay down beside him, leaning over to kiss him, idly stroking his side. "And I'm not close to done with you."

CHAPTER 3

After lazing around in bed far longer than he'd usually allow himself, Ryan quietly slipped away from Braxton, biting back a laugh when the young man rolled over and hugged his pillow tight. Damn, those disheveled, light brown curls, that slightly tanned, flawless skin, those thick lashes resting on cheeks that had the faintest touch of freckles...Ryan couldn't lie to himself, Braxton looked good in his bed. Yes, he wanted to fuck him again, but that wasn't why he hadn't handed him cab fare yet.

Maybe he'd been working too much and the company was nice. Hell, he couldn't remember the last time he'd spent time with anyone outside of work. Sure, he had lunch with his sister now and then, but Laura being an officer at the same station meant they didn't talk about much besides work and her relationship.

He was happy for her, he really was, but he couldn't imagine managing his job and a person who'd expect time and attention every single day. Or even a few times a week. He'd tried dating, years ago, and no matter how much effort he'd put in it hadn't been enough. He'd figured dating another detective would be easier, that since they both knew the lifestyle their limited time together would be special. And it had been special to him.

To Detective Simon Ackman, limited time and being closeted meant an opportunity to...explore his other options. How fucking cliché that Ryan had caught Simon fucking some random guy on a night he'd finished early and showed up to surprise his boyfriend.

Almost two years of trying to find a balance between work and a relationship, only to have it thrown in his face that Simon needed more. Of course, he should have communicated as much —Ryan refused to take all the blame for how badly things had ended between them—but the point was, after being hurt and angry, he realized he simply didn't have the time or energy to invest in the kind of relationship he wanted.

He'd have known he couldn't trust Simon if he'd treated him like he did the subs he played with at the clubs. They'd only done light kink though and Ryan hadn't had the experience he'd developed since. Five year later and whenever he saw Simon he wondered how he'd missed how fake the man's smile was. The way his gaze shifted before he told lie after lie to make himself look good. How he strategically made friends and used them for his own gain.

For two years he'd managed to hide that side of himself from Ryan.

Or maybe Ryan had been so infatuated with the idea of being in love he'd refused to see it. He wasn't that man anymore and never would be again.

Spending a few hours making sure a sub wasn't being honest with his limits and emotions was one thing and he only allowed himself to play that way once or twice a month. Picking up someone for a quick, no-strings-attached fuck was simpler.

Except when it came to someone like Braxton. Because he

could see himself enjoying Braxton at the club. Drawing out his submissive side, working over that body Ryan couldn't tear his eyes away from with a flogger, tying him up and edging him until he was crying and begging in that sweet voice of his.

Which will never happen.

At the BDSM club Ryan only scened with experienced subs—for the same reason he avoided taking home gaybies with more hormones than common sense. Braxton had needed this though. Needed the kind of experience that made having to hide who he was were a little easier to bear. From what Ryan knew of the hockey team the young man likely played for, The Dartmouth Cobras, there were enough players out and proud that it should've been easy for Braxton to claim his identity.

Why hadn't he?

Not the kind of question you can ask without confusing the kid. Keep it about sex. Set his standards high. He'll be better for it.

A bit arrogant to think he'd have that kind of impact, but he honestly hoped he would. Braxton was a good guy. He deserved to be happy.

No harm in letting him rest a bit before enjoying the bit of time they had left, though. Ryan left the room quietly, taking a quick shower before heading to the kitchen in his thick black robe to grab a beer. He'd gone to the club not expecting to have more than one drink, since he'd driven there, but now that he was home and overthinking absolutely everything, he could afford to mellow out.

He was just starting to feel the pleasant buzz as he polished off one beer and opened another when Braxton padded into the room. Completely naked.

Ryan's lips curved. Not only was Braxton fucking nice too look at, but if he had been Ryan's submissive, this was how he'd be every time they were alone. That he'd come by the urge naturally messed with Ryan's determination to remain detached.

"Sorry for passing out on you. I didn't mean to waste the whole night sleeping." Braxton rested his hip against the edge of the table, close enough for Ryan to grab him, without being so close he demanded attention. His expression was soft, as though he was still half-asleep. "Do you mind if I have one?"

Inclining his head and motioning to the fridge, Ryan kept his eyes on Braxton as he made his way over, the muscles in his tight, round ass making Ryan's mouth water. It took all his strength to remain in his seat when all he had to do was take two long strides across the room, pin Braxton against the closest hard surface, and slide his already fully recovered dick into that snug heat.

Instead, he waited for Braxton to pull out the only other chair at the small, round oak table and lifted his bottle in silent cheers. "No need to be sorry, I intended to wear you out." His lips slid into a smug smile as pink stained Braxton's cheeks. "I'm pleased that I succeeded."

"You should be. Usually takes at least a few shifts on the ice before I'm ready to slow down." Braxton took a long gulp of beer, then ducked his head. "As for sex, I've never been...well, after I'm just restless. I like knowing the girl enjoyed herself, but I feel bad pretending I did too."

"Then stop." All right, that was enough beer. Ryan wouldn't help the young man by pretending things were that simple. But he couldn't help being frustrated at what Braxton was telling him. "I understand that you have an image to uphold, but does that really need to involve using women as some kind of front? They deserve better and so do you."

Nodding slowly, Braxton stared at his bottle. "I know, but I thought..." He sighed. "I have this friend and we've fooled around with some girls together. And I enjoy myself a lot when he's there. I figured if I kept doing that, it would be okay."

"But it hasn't been."

"No. He just thinks I like it and doesn't know I was into him and after tonight I'm thinking…it wasn't about him at all." Lifting his shoulders, Braxton wet his lips with his tongue and met Ryan's eyes. "Not that I wasn't attracted to him, I totally was. But he was safe and I could pretend I didn't want more."

"Now you know you do." Ryan reached out and took hold of Braxton's wrist, stroking along his pulse. "That's good. And I hope you remember that."

Lips curving slightly, Braxton shrugged again. "After my nap, the memory is a bit fuzzy."

Ryan spat out a laugh. Fuck, this was fun. He couldn't remember the last time he'd had this much fun talking to someone when there was sex involved.

He tugged at Braxton's wrist until the young man stood, then pulled him into his lap. With Braxton straddling him it was easier to focus on the moment and toss aside the idea of stealing more time. He couldn't afford to let the man get attached. He was already slipping himself and that would lead nowhere good.

Thankfully, Braxton being a brat gave him the perfect excuse to shift the topic back to why he was here. With the weight of the young man on his thighs, he let his hands curve around that sweet ass he still hadn't gotten enough of.

"Your memory is fuzzy, is it?" Ryan slid his fingers between Braxton's cheeks, then pressed them to the hole that was still slick from all the lube he'd used. He pressed two fingers in, curving them as Braxton let out a throaty moan. "Does this help?"

Braxton shuddered, his hot dick pressing against Ryan's stomach through the part in his robe. "It really does."

"Good. But I don't like to waste things. Finish your beer."

Ryan eased his fingers languorously in and out, pleased that Braxton didn't question him and shakily brought his beer to his lips. This wasn't about getting the man drunk, he hadn't had enough to feel more than relaxed. But he'd learn not to rush the moment. "You're not pretending for anyone now. You're simply here for me to play with. And I want to fuck you again."

"Yes please." Braxton rested his head on Ryan's shoulder, breathing hard. "Do you want me to ride your dick, because I can do that. I want to."

The sweet way he asked shredded the last bit of control Ryan had. His dick throbbed as he imagined how fucking good it would be to just give in and fill that sweet ass, but he wasn't so far gone he forgot using protection.

Between his regular blood tests and the ones Braxton likely had as a pro athlete, it likely wasn't needed, but that wasn't an example he wanted to set. Not when he had no intention of keeping the young man.

Damn it.

"Go to my room and grab some condoms." Ryan's breaths came a little easier when Braxton pushed away from him and hurried off. They were on the same page.

He just had to stick to the plan. Fuck and forget. It shouldn't be this difficult.

But when Braxton returned, kneeling between his thighs and giving him a look that might as well have been him asking 'May I, Sir?', it got harder to simply nod. To not see exactly what he was letting go by limiting this to one night.

Condom covering his dick, Ryan drew Braxton up over him, hands on Braxton's thighs as the young man positioned himself and eased down. He'd added more lube, making Ryan's dick slide into him faster than he'd intended, but when Braxton began to move, all he could do was lose himself in the other man's body.

"Fuck, that's nice." He wrapped his arms around Braxton's

waist when he tried to find a fast rhythm. "But slow down. Let me enjoy you."

"Are you?" Braxton's voice hitched as he caught his breath and brought his lips to Ryan's. "Because I want everything. You're giving me one night and it won't be enough."

Curving his hand around the back of Braxton's neck, he held the younger man's gaze. "It will be." He lifted Braxton by the hips and thrust up into him. "Stay with me. Right here. Feel what I'm doing to you. Take what I'm willing to give."

The position was too intimate. He kissed Braxton again, saw the tenderness in his eyes, and knew he had to regain control before he did real damage. Pleasure was one thing. He could give Braxton that. But he was crossing into dangerous territory.

Shoving his chair back he rose, still inside Braxton, and laid him over the table. He curved one hand around the nape of Braxton's neck and held him down as he fucked him, using his free hand to jerk Braxton off. He came as Braxton did, giving in to the pulsing grip around his dick.

Drawing away, he resisted the urge to hold Braxton, simply supporting him with a hand under his elbow until Braxton slumped into his seat. This had to be it. The way Braxton had spoken when Ryan had been deep inside him proved how bad the young man was at separating his emotions from sex. Which didn't have to be a bad thing.

Except with Ryan.

Still, he couldn't send Braxton home yet. He laughed when Braxton gave him a sleepy smile and brought the man back to his bed. Fucked him one last time when they were both half asleep because he couldn't resist. Let himself cherish the final moments when Braxton got up before him and fixed a horrible cup of coffee. He even choked down every last sip.

Then he got dressed and made the excuse that he had to get

to work. Which he didn't. He wouldn't have been at the club if he had to work today.

But he knew his limits. And he'd reached them.

Thankfully, Braxton didn't argue when he offered to drive him home. Didn't say a word until they were there.

By that time, Ryan had accepted this would be the last time they ever spoke.

But he'd never forget that smile. And couldn't help wish he didn't have to.

"Thanks for the ride." Braxton walked around the car to the driver's side, chewing on his bottom lip. He didn't want this to be over. He liked Ryan. A lot. And not just because the sex had been amazing.

He liked talking to Ryan. He liked the way Ryan took over and made him feel comfortable in his own skin. Every inch of his body smelled like the man, like he'd left his mark, and he couldn't let that go.

"I should've called you a cab." Ryan's tone was distant, and he wouldn't meet Braxton's eyes. He'd meant it when he said tonight was a one-time thing.

But he was wrong.

It wasn't meant to be. Maybe Ryan thought he was too young. Too inexperienced. He was a cop, so he was probably worried about shit Braxton hadn't thought of yet, but they could work on that.

He leaned in, stealing a quick kiss and smiling against Ryan's lips. "I'll call you."

"Sure." Ryan looked away. "Take care, Braxton. Remember what I said."

"I will." Braxton stepped away from the curb. Sighed as Ryan pulled out and drove away. He wasn't good at this. He had no idea what to do next. But he'd figure it out.

Ryan didn't want to forget him, but he had this whole idea of how things should go. An awesome night. Nothing complicated. Just memories.

Could he stick to that if they saw one another again?

Braxton didn't know. But he would damn well find out.

Only one problem.

He didn't have Ryan's number. And calling 911 to get it probably wouldn't go over well. He didn't want to push too hard, but he already knew Ryan would be impossible to forget.

Maybe Ryan could forget him easily, but he doubted it. He smiled as he quietly let himself into the apartment he shared with a teammate. He couldn't share what had happened last night with anyone, but it stuck with him as he took a shower, then crawled into bed. As he dreamt of Ryan holding him, even though he wasn't sure the man had actually done it.

Didn't matter. There would be a next time. There had to be.

He had to believe the next time Ryan saw him, he'd want more. He'd admit they had something worth exploring. First, he had to make sure there'd be a next time.

But he wasn't too worried. He'd find a way. He hadn't become a professional hockey player by letting opportunities slip away. And he knew an opportunity when he saw it.

This definitely fit.

CHAPTER 4

Two weeks and Braxton still hadn't figured out how to get in touch with Ryan. He'd stopped by the club, ignoring all the other men who hit on him and tried to watch the dancers on stage rather than the doors, but that got him nowhere. Terry brought him drinks and kept the creepy dudes that hung around back, giving Braxton this pitying look before making small talk.

For the first night anyway.

On the second night, near closing time, he finally pulled out the stool next to Braxton and sat down, facing him. "Honey, I hate seeing you waiting on that man. And I say that as his friend. He's on a big case right now, so he won't be back for a while, but you need to know that when he does start coming again, he's not going to give you what you want."

Braxton frowned down at his glass full of ice, avoiding Terry's concerned gaze. "You have no idea what I want."

"It's more than sex or you'd notice the hot guys I keep sending your way." Terry let out an irritated huff when Braxton laughed. "It's not funny. You're a sweet kid—yes, I know you're not a child." He rolled his eyes at Braxton's glare. "But you are young. And you're infatuated with Ryan. This will only end in heartache."

Even knowing Terry for just a short time, Braxton had gotten used to how dramatic he was about everything. But he didn't have many friends outside of the team and he considered the flamboyant server one of them. There was no reason to have the guy worrying for nothing.

As the lights in the almost empty club came on, he reached out and patted Terry's hand. "I hear you, I promise. And I'm going on the road starting tomorrow, so I won't have time to obsess over Ryan. Not that I really have been, I just…there was something between us."

Terry's lips slanted. "He fucked you good and now you're stuck pretending you're into girls again." Terry let out a heavy sigh. "I've seen the pictures of you with all those gorgeous models. You put on a good act, I'll give you that."

"I have to."

"Maybe you don't, but you're not ready to come out publicly yet and I get that. This is where you come when you're tired of hiding who you are." Terry stood as Braxton did, walking with him to the door where his husband was letting out the last of the club's patrons. "And you're more than welcome. But you should consider that Ryan represents a kind of freedom you've never felt before, like this place does. You can have that anywhere, Braxton. With anyone."

Braxton hesitated, then shook his head. "I don't think I can."

"Have you tried?"

Those words stuck with Braxton long after he got home, lying in bed and trying to get enough sleep so he'd be up to the tough road trip coming up. Things had been weird in the locker room lately, what with the rookies who'd been brought up to replace three suspended players. He did his best to avoid those guys, but they were obnoxious, homophobic assholes and he couldn't stop tensing up whenever they walked into a room.

Part of him wondered if they could see the difference in him since he'd been with Ryan. They constantly joked about him being a pretty boy and liking cock, even though he'd been spending more time with the puck bunnies Hunt always seemed to find at a moment's notice. Which happened more and more often, almost as though Hunt had noticed something too and was trying to protect him.

Nothing had really changed, but he still felt like he had 'queer' written on his forehead. Even his agent had gotten more uptight about him being single and asked if there was a girl he could spend time with—or at least get a few photos with so people might assume they were together.

So no, Braxton hadn't tried being with another guy. How could he?

Wanting to be with Ryan isn't from a lack of options.

Or...was it?

The next afternoon he struggled to focus as he hit the ice with the rest of the team for practice. In the locker room, he hurried to shower and change, ignoring the rookie, Spooner, who dropped a bar of soap in front of him, whispering 'You're welcome' when Braxton bent down to pick it up.

Team policy against discrimination would have the rookie taking another round of sensitivity training if Braxton reported him, but he couldn't draw that kind of attention to himself. If he complained, Coach would wonder why he was taking the little jabs so personally. His contract was up at the end of the season and the only way he'd get signed to a longer one is if he didn't make waves and proved he was an asset to the team.

Sucked not being able to talk to anyone about it though. When the guys caught the rookies talking shit, they stuck up for him, but they couldn't be there all the time. As much as some tried—Hunt most of all—he had to deal with the fuckers on his own.

Mostly by ignoring them and hoping they got bored.

Speaking of which, he needed to get the hell out of the locker room. Fully dressed, he'd sat there thinking for so long the team had cleared out. Except for the rookies.

He grabbed his sports bag and started for the door. Spooner stood, blocking his path.

The door opened and Tyler Vanek, whose suspension was finally over, gave Spooner a cold look until he got out of Braxton's way. Dismissing the rookie, Vanek grinned at Braxton. "Hey, Richards! Saw you on the ice the other night fucking killing it! You were playing with Zovko and some rando who couldn't pass for shit, but I was impressed. Hopefully Coach starts giving you more playing time."

Spooner's face reddened. He shot Braxton a glare that promised revenge, but seriously, what could he do when he'd be sent back down to the minors starting tomorrow? Braxton ignored him and followed Vanek out to the player's lounge.

"We lost, but thanks anyway. It'll be good to have you back."

"Don't I know it." Vanek walked with him through the parking garage exit, letting out a low whistle when Braxton pulled out his keys and pressed the remote starter for his car. "Holy shit, kid. Nice ride!"

Braxton's cheeks heated and he shrugged as Vanek circled his new, gunmetal black Zenvo ST1, clear admiration in his eyes. The same expression Braxton probably had when he'd been checking out cars and the owner of the shop had brought him to look at this one.

"I can't really afford this." Braxton brushed his fingers along the hood of the car, voice barely above a whisper. "But…"

"You're a professional hockey player who'll be getting a big contract next year. I'm sure you'll manage."

Can I? Braxton swallowed hard. He didn't pay much in rent, sharing a small condo with another player who owned the place. He'd tried saving up a bit, but his agent was always on his back about wearing nice, expensive suits and 'looking the part'.

Maybe a car like this would get the man off his case.

"I guess I'd have to see if the bank would approve or whatever?" Shit, why had he come here alone? One of his teammates likely would've come with him, only he didn't feel close enough to anyone besides Hunt to ask. And all Hunt's money was managed by his father, so he didn't get to buy fun stuff at all.

Bringing him along would be like rubbing it in his face.

The car salesman, who'd introduced himself as Erik Patterson, gave Braxton a smile that was both encouraging, and understanding. "Your first new car is a big deal, son. Would you feel better if you had a parent here? Or maybe a friend you could talk this over with?"

Braxton shook his head. "Both my parents are enlisted. My dad shipped out last month and my mom's been running training exercises in the Ukraine for the past year."

"That's impressive. I thank them both for their service." Mr. Patterson stroked his jaw. "Let me tell you what I'll tell my own boy when he's your age. A car like this is a good investment. You can tell a lot about a man by the car he drives and this one says you're successful and have good taste. You're on the road a lot, so she'll be kept in mint condition, only being used to make an impact now and then. In a few years you could sell her when you're ready to settle down—assuming you're not considering doing so already."

For some reason, that made him think of Ryan. Who'd disappeared and seemed to think he was too young to be serious about anything. He might want to see the man again, more than anything, but he also wanted to prove him wrong.

Braxton was old enough to know what he wanted.

And right now he wanted this damn car.

He met Mr. Patterson's eyes. "Show me where to sign."

The payments on the car, and the insurance he hadn't considered, were going to bury him if he didn't get a good contract soon. Seeing the actual numbers kept him up at night and he was pretty sure he'd made a horrible mistake.

But he forced a smile as Vanek stepped up to his side. "Thanks. It's the only one in the Maritimes. Pricey, but fucking worth it."

"I'd say." Vanek let out a heavy sigh. "I love my car, but sometimes I wish I could just collect them, you know? But after being out of commission for so long, I try not to be stupid with my money. Not saying you were, but that's some fucking confidence. Your agent must be a damn good negotiator."

"Yeah..." Braxton wasn't sure how to respond to that. His agent wasn't bad, but he seemed more concerned with Braxton having the right image than actually getting him brand deals or even talking about his new contract.

A familiar voice jerked Braxton away from his thoughts and his lips parted as Ryan stepped into view with Laura Tallent, one of the two women in Tyler's poly relationship. Laura was a cop, so it wasn't a huge surprise that she knew Ryan.

But he hadn't been expecting to see either of them here.

"...was there anything else on the security footage that we should look into?" Ryan didn't seem to notice Braxton standing there as he turned to face Laura. "Nothing was stolen, so I assume the concern is the player's safety?"

"There was nothing concrete, just a break-in that didn't set off the alarm. The perp took off the second someone came to investigate after catching them on camera and there was no way to identify them." Laura took a few notes, motioning toward the round camera fixture imbedded in the cement ceiling above. "Security was already tight, but it's been updated."

"Good. Well, I'll file a report and have a team look into it, as well as increase patrols in the area. You can take the lead on this one, you're already familiar with the case." Ryan glanced over at Braxton and Vanek, his tone completely detached. "Have either of you seen anything suspicious?"

Braxton quickly shook his head.

Vanek frowned. "No, but should we be worried?"

Focusing on Vanek, Ryan's expression softened. "Not at all. As Officer Tallent pointed out, you have good security. This is simply precaution."

"Okay, cool." Vanek nudged Braxton with his elbow. "Feel like giving me a ride? You can't show me a car like that and force me to walk home."

Braxton grinned, looking across the parking lot to where the only other car, which belonged to Vanek, was parked. "Nice try."

"Oh fine, but next time?"

"Sure." Braxton wouldn't have minded bringing Vanek for a drive now, but Ryan was here. He finally had a chance to talk to him.

But he couldn't in front of his teammate. He liked Vanek, but he didn't know him well enough to risk exposing himself. And there was no way he could pretend there was nothing going on between him and Ryan.

Taking his time stuffing his sports bag in the trunk, Braxton waited until Vanek was gone before looking for Ryan again. His pulse raced when he saw him standing alone at the far end of the lot, Laura nowhere to be seen.

Cutting across the long expanse as fast as he could without running, he approached Ryan, hesitating when the man went perfectly still.

"This isn't a good time, Braxton."

"Fine. But you said you'd call and you don't have my number." Braxton folded his arms over his chest, feeling foolish for even approaching the man. "I thought I should fix that."

"Did you?" Ryan turned, looking from Braxton, to the car, his lips thinning slightly. "I'm not sure what was unclear about our last exchange. We had fun, but this—" He motioned from himself, to Braxton, "—doesn't work. Our lifestyles don't mesh. Even if I was interested in a relationship, it wouldn't be with a man almost fourteen years younger than me who lacks basic common sense."

Braxton's jaw hardened. "How do you figure?"

"A million dollar car. Who told you that was a good idea?" Ryan lifted a hand and shook his head. "You know what, it doesn't matter. It's none of my business. But whatever you think you want from me, you can find somewhere else."

Taking a step back, Braxton stared at the other man. "Fuck, I wasn't gonna ask you to marry me. Maybe you think I'm pathetic or—"

"I don't think that."

"Then what?"

"Braxton…" Ryan pressed his eyes shut and rubbed his hand over his face. "We can't have this conversation now. I'm tempted to tell you all the reasons that car was a mistake. And why you should stop going to that club when you still don't know what you want."

Warmth filled Braxton's chest as he considered Ryan's words. He'd been checking up on Braxton. Knew he'd been going to the club. As much as he tried to deny it, he cared. He wanted Braxton in his life.

Braxton just had to find a way to prove he fit there.

And he would.

"I'll take the lecture. But you're right, you're working and you can't give it to me now. So call me when you can."

One brow arched, Ryan met his eyes. "You're incorrigible."

"No, I take people at their word. And you said you'd call."

"Fine." Ryan pulled out a notepad and pen. "Give me your

number. Then get out of here before I forget I'm on the clock and bend you over my knee."

"Now I'm confused." Braxton leaned close and lowered his voice. "Are you trying to get me to stay?"

Ryan chuckled. "No, brat. You need to leave. But clearly you won't let this go until we talk, so we shall. But don't push me. If I decide you need to be punished, you will not enjoy it."

"Kinky."

"Your number, Braxton."

Taking the hint, Braxton gave Ryan his number, chewing on his bottom lip when Ryan fixed him with a heated stare. He'd expected this to be a lot harder, but even after two weeks, a few minutes with Ryan showed him nothing had changed.

And as much as Ryan wanted to deny it, they weren't done.

Not even close.

CHAPTER 5

"Did the kid give you anything useful?"

Sitting in the passage seat of his sister's unit, Ryan schooled his features and shook his head. Laura knew him too well for him to say much until he had his own thoughts sorted out and he wasn't even close. What the fuck had he been thinking, tagging along on one of her cases to the damn place where Braxton played and practiced? He'd known there was a chance he'd see the man.

Self-denial wasn't usually his thing. Maybe he'd wanted to see Braxton.

But it had been a mistake, because now he couldn't get the guy out of his head. He'd been doing fine, focusing on work and leaving the past in the past where it belonged. His time with Braxton had to be nothing but a memorable night.

He hadn't counted on how memorable, but he'd compartmentalized any wayward emotions as he always did, refusing to let the *'what ifs'* sink in.

Trying to focus on the paperwork in his lap, he was grateful when Laura continued speaking, accepting his nod as answer enough. "I'm happy he and Tyler didn't stick around. I was hoping not to see any of the players. I swear our captain gives me any cases involving the team just to mess with me."

Ryan frowned and glanced over at his sister. "Why would he do that?"

Laura's expression hardened. "Because he suspects my relationship is more…complicated than I let off. He knows I'm with Chicklet, but Tyler's always around. Both he and Chicklet are discreet, but there's this undercurrent… It's hard to explain. And I have no intention of ever doing so. But while the captain won't risk the PR mess of making things difficult because I'm a lesbian, he has no problem using how uncomfortable I am around the team against me."

"Why are you uncomfortable around them?" Ryan liked Laura's girlfriend, Chicklet, and other than being young and unruly, Chicklet's boyfriend, Tyler, seemed harmless enough.

But 'complicated' was putting it lightly. Laura was a damn fine officer, and had managed to balance her relationship and her job for years. Tyler becoming part of it seemed to be getting to her more and more, but she didn't open up much about why. The young man had gotten himself arrested, which obviously didn't help, and yet, she'd mentioned the team.

His jaw hardened. He'd agreed not to give Tyler the big brother third degree because the man and Laura weren't technically involved, but like hell would Ryan let any of those other assholes mess with his sister. He might be having a chat with the police captain while he was at it.

"Stop it, Ryan." Laura let out a light laugh and backhanded his shoulder. "I can already see you going into protective mode. I'm fine. I just have no interest in dealing with a bunch of athletes with big salaries and a total disregard for the rules. They have the money to get out of whatever bullshit they pull, to throw around on expensive cars and any random thing they might want. I can't relate, even while having one of them in my own home."

Nodding slowly, Ryan thought back on Braxton with his outrageous car and how, in that moment, he'd realized they lived two completely different lifestyles. That didn't mesh.

He could have fun with Braxton for a little while, but then what? The man might insist he didn't want anything serious—did he really mean it?

There was only one way to find out. He'd promised to talk to Braxton, and he would.

As soon as he figured out how to lay the ground rules. The last thing he wanted was to be stuck in a situation like Laura was in. As a submissive, maybe she didn't feel she had as much of a say. Or that she'd waited too long to bring it up with Chicklet now. So far she hadn't wanted to discuss it, but when she was, he'd gently nudge her toward better communicating her needs.

And wish Chicklet the best of luck because he couldn't imagine trying to manage two submissives.

He still wasn't sure he wanted *one.*

Not that he could tell if Braxton would be into the lifestyle at all. If he wasn't that would make keeping things short term easy. If he was…

No. Still no.

Relationships weren't for Ryan. But he might consider playing with Braxton for a little while if the man could deal with hooking up now and then. If he didn't get attached.

Ryan had managed when he'd been Braxton's age. Sure, he'd had his moments when he looked at the older man by his side and imagined an ideal future, but his life had revolved around school and joining the police force. Braxton's revolved around playing professional hockey.

If nothing else, that might be the one reason they could have something casual. Something enjoyable for them both.

He'd find out soon enough.

The week had finally come to an end. Ryan never watched the clock, but after the hours of paperwork he'd put in after what seemed like nonstop chaos, he was eager to get his tired ass home. Days like this had been nothing when he was in his twenties, and he was still in good shape in his mid-thirties, but the excited rush of it all had long passed.

He could use a few days off. Maybe at his parent's place, away from the city. Time to clear his head and stop hearing the sound of sirens, the screams of perps who insisted they were innocent, the smell of smoke which had become far too familiar with the most recent string of arson cases.

Movement at his side drew his attention away from his last file and he smiled as Laura came to stand beside him. She'd had a rough week too. Hopefully, he could convince her to come with him to visit their parents. He couldn't remember the last time she'd taken more than a day off.

Before he could say a word, she held out her phone.

"The hockey player you spoke to in the parking lot earlier this week. He wants to talk to you."

She sounded so worn out it took a moment for her words to register over his concern. Then he stared at the phone.

Braxton had...called his sister?

What. The. Actual. Fuck?

He took the phone. Tried his best to tamp down his rage. Maybe Braxton had a good reason to call. Had something happened at the forum? Another break in?

It better be a goddamn break in. Or someone better be dying.

"Hello?" His tone was calm. Level. Maybe a bit hard, but he was doing his best not to assume the worst.

"Uh...hey." Braxton hesitated. "This was a mistake."

"Was it now?" Ryan's jaw clenched. Laura was still close, so he had to make the call sound normal. Unimportant. "Is there any new information that I should be aware of?"

"Huh?"

Think, Hamilton. What could he be calling about that would make sense to your sister? He leaned back in his chair, trying to release the tension in his shoulders and relax his voice. "Are you sure your bike was there the whole time?"

"I..." Braxton cleared his throat. "I'm sorry. I shouldn't have called, but I was waiting to hear from you."

"I see." Ryan hadn't considered the young man might be watching his phone all week, expecting it to ring. Maybe he should have, but he'd convinced himself they were on the same page.

I was so fucking wrong.

"Did you even mean it when you said you'd call? If you didn't, why didn't you just tell me to fuck off? I can take a hint you know." Braxton sounded irritated by the long pause. "I just... Shit. You're pissed now, aren't you?"

Damn right he was, but he couldn't say that. Not now. Probably not ever. He'd already led Braxton on without meaning to.

But Braxton said he could take a hint. So he'd give him that.

"I understand, but there's not much I can do. It isn't my department. If we find your bike, you'll hear from us. But it seems unlikely at this point." Was that too vague? Fuck, he didn't need this shit in his life. Braxton wanted more than he could give. He didn't want to hurt the kid, but they were done. "Please don't call this number again. There's a proper procedure to follow. If you need an update, you'll have to ask someone else."

The line was so quiet for so long Ryan wondered if Braxton had hung up. That would be best. A clean cut. There was nothing more to say.

Then he heard a deep breath. "If I had waited, would you have called me?"

Pressing his eyes shut, Ryan sighed. Honesty might help Braxton with his next relationship. Or…well, not like they'd had a relationship, but this phone call had destroyed the chance they could have anything.

"Yes. But that doesn't matter now." Ryan shot his sister a quick smile at her concerned look. "Goodbye."

CHAPTER 6

The best thing Braxton could do was forget about Ryan, but he couldn't. He'd messed up by calling him. He should've waited.

Instead, he'd told Vanek he wanted to ask the detective they'd seen at the forum for some more information—which got him a weird look from his teammate, but the man had simply given him Laura's number. What Braxton had expected from the call, he couldn't say.

Not Ryan shutting him down, that was for sure.

So what now? He groaned as he pushed himself to catch up with White, who he'd called that morning, asking if the man wanted to go for a run. Hunt had been making himself scarce ever since things in the locker room had gotten tense and comments about people being gay were whispered more often. Braxton hoped he hadn't done anything to freak his friend out.

Yeah, he'd had a crush on Hunt, but as far as he knew, the man was straight. He wouldn't intentionally do anything to make him uncomfortable and their friendship meant more than anything. Focusing on Ryan, on what he thought they might have was better.

But still pointless.

Maybe he was meant to be alone. Maybe Ryan was right and he should just have fun. Not think too much about with who. Not care if they ghosted him the next day.

"Pick up the pace rookie." White turned around, running backwards as he waited for Braxton to join him along the pier, which was almost completely cleared of snow. "You usually run with Hunt and he's a beast. You ain't hurting, are you?"

A little? But Braxton forced a smile, knowing that wasn't what White meant. "I'm good, just not sleeping as much as I should. Fucking excited to make the playoffs!"

"I hear you!" White grinned, facing forward again and slowing his pace to an easy jog. "Barely a week home and we're off on another road trip, but I love that shit. Except for the flying."

"Yeah, sucks that you hate it so much. I love the view, looking down and seeing a new city, knowing I get to experience things I wouldn't have gotten a chance to if I hadn't made it this far." Braxton smiled at the thought. As confusing as his personal life was, he'd always have hockey. He was good at hockey. Maybe not the best, but he could work on that.

And to be real, he didn't need any distractions. Not before the playoffs.

White slowed even more, reaching out to rub the back of Braxton's neck. "You're just getting started kid. And don't worry about me. Pisch gets me through the flights."

"Uh huh."

"What do you mean, 'uh huh'?" White frowned and let his hand fall to his side as he stopped. "He tries. I know I still look all fucked up, but it would be worse if he wasn't there."

"I know, man. It's just…" Braxton decided to drop it. 'It' being what he saw going on between White and Shawn Pischlar. For all he knew about relationships, he could be way off. And White didn't get subtleties, so teasing him was cruel. "It's nothing. I'm glad he can help you a bit at least."

Expression warming, as though talking about Pischlar made him happy, White nodded. "He really does. And I'm lucky he's so patient. I'm a mess."

"You are not. Come on, not being good on planes isn't—"

"I mean this." White gestured to the ankle monitor he had to wear for 'aggravated assault' after defending Pischlar from a bunch of homophobic assholes at a local gym. "Do you know how much paperwork the team had to do so I could travel with the team?" He hesitated. "Speaking of all that shit, I have to check in with the cop who's monitoring me to tell her where I'm gonna be on the road trip. Wanna come with?"

"Sure. I…I had a bike stolen and wanted to see if there was any news anyway."

Shit. What am I doing?

Showing up at the police station, he might see Ryan. And Ryan had made it clear they were done.

But…

Would he still think that if they were face to face? Last time Braxton had seen him, Ryan had relaxed after a bit. Still seemed interested. Maybe Braxton was wrong, but would it hurt to try, one last time? Wasn't like he was going out of his way. He was going with White.

If the man looked him in the eye and said what he did on the phone, Braxton would move on. He had to.

But he couldn't until he found some closure. Which might be ridiculous, he'd known the man for one night.

Still…that night meant something,

I can't let it go.

Not yet.

"Cool. Let's head back to my place and we'll drive over." White seemed so happy that he'd be coming that Braxton couldn't second guess himself.

They jogged back to White's place. He climbed in White's car.

And then considered staying in it when they pulled up in front of the police station.

Ryan was there. Right there with Chicklet. When White got out, Braxton did too. He sensed Ryan's eyes on him and his throat locked.

This is a huge mistake.

"I gotta see my house arrest lady to tell her where I'll be at during the road trip. She said she'd meet me here." White gestured to Braxton without looking over. "Kid wanted to come for the ride. He said he got his bike stolen last week and he reported it?"

"Not my department." Ryan's gaze was cutting as he frowned at Braxton. "I'm sure they told you they'd call?"

"But they didn't." Braxton ducked his head and scuffed his sneakers on the pavement. He prayed for the earth to swallow him whole. "Figured I'd hear something the next day."

"Well, you didn't." Ryan's tone went cold. "That should tell you something."

Avoiding Ryan's glare, Braxton stepped up to White's side. Spoke softly. "I'm gonna wait for you here. It's just a bike. I shouldn't be bugging them about it."

White's brow furrowed, but he nodded before heading inside.

Braxton slipped back into the passenger seat of the car and kept his head down. If things hadn't been clear before, they were now. Ryan wanted nothing to do with him. A night that had meant so much to Braxton was probably no different than any other for the man.

Completely humiliated, stomach turning, all Braxton could do was think about the game.

Think about the one place he mattered.

Because right now, with Ryan so close, with the sight of him reminding him of everything they'd done together…

He might as well be invisible.

And he didn't know how to pretend that was okay.

CHAPTER 7

Ryan's life had become one disaster after another. His sister was on administrative leave after shooting a drug dealer who'd attacked her with a knife. The leave was a good thing, she needed a break, but the way the internal investigator, Detective West, was treating her seemed personal.

Against Ryan.

He'd never thought his sister would get a hard time because he'd been a hotheaded rookie. Or because as a moody teen the last year of high school when their family had moved here, he'd fought West's younger brother a few times. Maybe even because he'd gotten up the ranks fast once he'd pulled his life together and the man fucking hated treating him as an equal.

Whatever the case, Laura didn't deserve to be targeted. And maybe the actual leave was all by the books, but what West had said while Laura had been finishing up the paperwork and turning in her badge and gun?

"She should be out soon, Hamilton. I must say I'm a little disappointed, though. I was hoping, since she's not a blood relative, that she didn't share your disregard for the rules." West pulled a pack of ciga-

rettes from his pocket, tapped one out, then brought it to his lips and lit the tip. "Apparently it runs in the family."

"You know damn well it was a clean kill, West." Ryan shoved away from the car, his jaw ticking as he considered how much damage the fucker could do to Laura's career. "You got a problem with me, don't take it out on her."

"Don't flatter yourself. I handled her no differently than I would any other officer. And she gets no special treatment for being your foster sister." West let out a puff of smoke with a laugh. "Please inform her a note from your mommy won't suffice for the psych eval."

He'd almost nailed the other man with a swift punch, but Chicklet had grabbed him and used her sharp wit as a weapon instead. The Domme had made West seem absolutely pathetic and Ryan realized getting himself suspended for hitting a fellow detective, no matter how satisfying, wouldn't do Laura any good. She needed him to be her strong, stable big brother, not the reckless boy he'd left behind.

His emotions were still raw though. And seeing Braxton hadn't helped. He'd thought he'd closed that particular door, but while he'd been waiting for Laura, suddenly Braxton was there.

A complication he couldn't handle.

Fucking handsome, looking so vulnerable part of Ryan told his sensible side to fuck off and cross the short distance and hold him. Take the pain out of his eyes. Explain why he couldn't be the person Braxton so clearly wanted him to be.

But there was still some hope in Braxton's eyes, hidden among the confusion. Hope that didn't belong there, not after the small bit of time they'd been together. Braxton was young, so maybe Ryan had been wrong about what he actually needed. Maybe he was ready for a relationship. Maybe he needed a connection with whoever he had sex with. Maybe being his first lover—the first he didn't have to pretend with—had him feeling there was a connection between them.

Ryan wouldn't lie to himself and say he was completely immune to Braxton. He could easily get wrapped up in the man. Forget the age difference, or how little time he had to devote to a relationship. Or how little desire...

No, desire definitely wasn't a problem. He'd take Braxton back into his bed in a second. See if he looked as hot on his knees wearing a collar as Ryan imagined.

None of that mattered. Braxton was already in too deep, much too fast. Ryan would hurt him, either now or later.

Better it be now.

The young man would recover.

First, he had to understand there was nothing here for him. Even if Ryan had to make Braxton hate him to do it. Which shouldn't be hard. All Ryan had to do was let out all his anger and frustrations over the past few days. Be as cold and cutting as possible, without revealing too much to Chicklet who'd been waiting with him for Laura, or White who was actually there for a reason.

He made it about the bike. Braxton would know exactly what he really meant. White would be fooled. Chicklet...unlikely, but she'd respect his privacy.

A good plan, but Braxton's crushed expression was like a kick in the guts. Looking away from him took every bit of strength Ryan had, but he did it. All that mattered was giving Braxton back the power he'd so innocently handed over. Forcing him to harden his heart a little.

He'd need it as he tried to find a balance in his life between being who he really was, and who he had to pretend to be in front of the cameras.

Once Braxton and White were gone, Chicklet gave Ryan a level look that spoke volumes.

He shook his head. "None of your business."

"Got it."

Maybe she did, but that didn't change what she hadn't said.

He heard it loud and clear.

"You're an asshole."

His jaw clenched as he did his best to push Braxton out of his mind so he could focus on Laura. Who needed him more.

Not that it changed anything.

Chicklet was right.

CHAPTER 8

Another road trip and the timing was perfect. Braxton couldn't keep avoiding everyone and everything because his emotions were a wreck and the game gave him something good to focus on.

Kinda…

The tension in the locker room had diminished now that the 'Trouble Triplets' were back and the asshole rookies were gone, but there was still this uncomfortable undertone that seemed to hover around the inner circle of the team. He hadn't noticed it as much just seeing the guys at games and practice, but on the road it was hard to ignore.

Scott Demyan and his partner, Zachory Pearce, were being weird with one another and he couldn't stand it. Zach was the first openly gay player on the team, out to the media and everything, and seeing things go well for him had given Braxton hope. Now?

All he could see was how messy things could get.

Things weren't all bad though. Over the past few days, White had been spending more time with Braxton, which was freakin' awesome. The man was tough and ruggedly handsome and fun to be around. As far as Braxton knew, White was straight, but the looks he gave his best friend, Shawn Pischlar, made him wonder sometimes.

White hadn't been with Pisch much lately, instead giving Braxton pointers on the ice and even teaching him how to fight. Which was a good distraction from how weird Hunt was acting.

Braxton's roommate had met a chick and moved out, so he figured he'd offer Hunt the spare room. The guy was staying in a cheap apartment, pretty isolated aside from regular calls and visits from his overbearing father. Even though they'd grown a bit distant, Braxton figured they were still friends and the company would be nice.

Only, Hunt wasn't…great company. He had a schedule his dad made for him that he followed, a diet he pushed on Braxton, and they hardly spoke at all anymore. Braxton got dedication to the game, but every single minute of every day? Hell, he felt guilty sitting down to watch TV with Hunt on the treadmill in the spare room he'd set up as a home gym. He let Hunt take over the groceries and couldn't stand half the food in his fridge.

Being on the road meant a change of pace and hopefully some normal food. White had been asking him how he'd been eating, so it must be obvious Braxton had lost weight over the past two weeks. Not enough for the trainers to get on his case yet, but that would come next.

Between flavorless food he couldn't stomach, the awkwardness he'd invited into his home, and just feeling really low lately, Braxton had dropped almost ten pounds. And he wasn't huge to begin with. He pushed himself hard to make sure his performance didn't suffer, but he was starting to get tired whenever he wasn't on the ice. The rush of adrenalin wasn't there to keep him going. He was just sorta…going through the motions of every day.

He refused to believe Ryan giving him the cold shoulder had anything to do with him being so damn miserable. Who cared if he couldn't stop thinking about the man? What did it matter that their bit of time together played over and over in his head? That he'd gone from feeling good about a hidden side of himself to… simply hiding again?

Damn it, he couldn't fool himself completely though. He pictured Ryan's smile. His voice, rough with pleasure, or firm with disapproval and wished he could go back to before he'd fucked everything up. Maybe if he'd slowed down he could've proved to Ryan he wasn't a complete disaster. They could've had that chat.

Back at the hotel, carrying his overnight bag, Braxton let out a heavy sigh. The heavy weight of White's arm around his neck almost knocked him over.

"Things are better, kid. We've had a few losses, but that team-building exercise was cool, right?"

"It was. And hell, we won against Philly. So…yay?" Braxton shrugged. "Sorry, I'm just…worn out I guess."

"You want me to head back to my room then? I enjoy hanging out, but not if it's messing with your sleep."

Braxton frowned and shook his head. He didn't want to be alone. The vet he'd originally been roomed with, one of their defensemen, Mirek Brends, was the ideal player and he made Braxton feel like a loser for not wanting to hit the sack at precisely 11:30PM every night. Not because anything he said or did, really, but he reminded Braxton a bit of Ryan. What Ryan would probably expect from him. That orderly, responsible life where Braxton didn't fit. This time, he'd gotten his own room and it was a relief. He was tired enough to want to go right there, but he wasn't ready to crash yet.

Hanging out with White and having a few beers was the break in the routine he needed. He couldn't let go of the one thing he had besides the game. The one person who actually seemed to like being around him.

He shot White an amused smile as he turned around, walking backwards to the elevator. "Your turn to pay for beer. You punking out on me?"

White snorted. "Not a chance. But you've got to promise to eat too, all right? Gotta gain back some of that weight you lost because of our crazy rookie goalie."

As they stepped onto the elevator, Braxton shoved his hands into his pockets. "He's not…crazy. I don't know, he's dedicated and all, but it's too much sometimes. I care about him, but I'm not sure I'm a good friend."

White frowned at him, folding his arms over his chest and leaning against the wall as the elevator started up. "You let him pick every meal, and you're all patient when he goes from being protective to shutting you out. How is that not being a good friend?"

Braxton shrugged, not sure what to say. He almost wished he could go back to admiring Hunt and being close without things being weird. But Hunt acted like a pat on the shoulder was pushing his new limits. Like he didn't even know how to talk to Braxton anymore.

Losing both Ryan and Hunt? Braxton was just…done. He preferred White's straightforward way of dealing with the world. He seemed happy, even if things were weird between him and Pisch. Maybe he could give Braxton some tips on how to shut the complicated shit out.

"Hey, I was thinking…" White rubbed his jaw as they got off the elevator. "There were a few chicks down there in the hotel restaurant that seemed interested. One gave me her number. She works here and was on break. If you want maybe we could invite her and her friends to my room."

Throat locking, Braxton did his best to keep his expression

neutral. He hadn't wanted this with White. He'd had enough of trying to be good with girls for Hunt. He always felt like shit when he couldn't get hard and a woman wondered if she'd done something wrong. With Hunt he'd been able to focus on how attracted he was to the man and forget how wrong every touch was. How much he wished they were alone.

"Drinks first." He followed White into the room and collapsed on his bed, one arm over his eyes. "Then…whatever."

"Dude, what's going on with you?" White dropped onto the bed beside him, reaching for the phone. He ordered some burgers, a case of beer and a bottle of whiskey without waiting for Braxton's answer. After he hung up he turned on his side, frowning. "Hey…that whole thing with the bike? Did you ever get that worked out?"

Braxton let out a strained laugh. He almost wished White knew the bike thing was a cover, but he wasn't sure the man would get why things with Ryan were still eating at him.

"No, the bike thing is…over I guess. I'll probably never see it again."

"That really sucks."

"Yeah." There really wasn't much else to say. Braxton was relieved when the food and drinks got there. He laughed at the look White gave him when he opened his burger and took the pickles out. He couldn't stand the things, but he had a feeling White wanted to make sure he ate.

He did. Both of his hamburgers and some fries before he started drinking.

The TV and whatever was music playing became background noise. He clinked his shot glass with White's, then downed his third shot. Nodded when White said they should slow down and have some beer. His head was nice and numb, and they didn't have another game for two days, but he didn't want to get sick.

Sitting at the round table near the window, Braxton snacked

on his cooling fries, then took a sip of his second beer. He watched White pace the room, arching a brow when White poured them each another shot.

"I'm a bad influence." White groaned, throwing back the shot and staring at his phone. "Fuck, why does everyone talk about me and Pisch so much? He's my friend. That's…that's it."

Braxton took his own shot, then shrugged. "If it makes you feel any better, I checked out some fanfic online and people fantasize about full out team gangbangs. I laughed at first, but then…not gonna lie, some of it was hot."

"Really?" White brought the bottle to his lips, not even bothering with a glass anymore. "Where are they getting those ideas from, though? I mean, half the guys on the team are married."

"Not quite half, but I don't think it matters. Those teens are trying to see something that's like them, you know?" Braxton gulped down his beer. Considered asking White for the whiskey, then settled on more beer. Which he was probably going to regret. "I used to look for that a lot."

Shut up! What are you doing?

He wasn't sure anymore. Watching White tug at his tie, he swallowed hard. All the times he'd been alone with White, he'd fought really hard to be cool. To say the right things. To act the right way. He didn't need to think of all those muscles, all that strength. Didn't need to wonder if White was interested, because he wasn't. Obviously, he wasn't.

But…but what if I'm wrong?

He pushed away from the table and went to the wonderful bed where he could sleep everything off and tomorrow things could go back to normal.

Normal like they'd been with Hunt before the man somehow figured out the chicks they hit on were doing nothing for him. Hunt must have noticed. Why else was he acting like a stranger? Braxton had figured out his crush wasn't going anywhere, but things still weren't completely okay. He had to fix that. He wanted his friend back.

You're fucking wasted.

He flopped an arm over his eyes. "I think that last shot was a mistake."

"Yeah." Ian sat on the edge of the bed. "You okay?"

"I guess." Braxton sighed, something inside him breaking open. He couldn't hold back anymore. "I just…fuck, I can't do this anymore. I keep hanging out with Hunt, and I love the man, but he doesn't get me."

White dropped onto the bed beside Richards. "What do you mean?"

"I'm gay. Like, totally, completely, into guys." Richards' stomach clenched as he turned his head, expecting White to tell him to get lost. He bit his bottom lip. "Go if you want. I know I shouldn't have said that."

"Why? I don't care who you fuck." Ian pressed his eyes shut. "I'm straight. Or I think I am. I don't know. It's fucking confusing."

"Is it? I don't think I've ever been confused." Richards rose up on his elbow, feeling a bit more comfortable opening up after White's confession. "Like, I've tried stuff with girls, but just because I thought I should. But when me and Hunt fool around with chicks, they don't get me hard. And that's where it's fucked up. We shared a chick once and…well, I was thinking about him the whole time. And I know he'd hate me if he knew."

"I don't think he'd hate you, but…maybe you're just into him? Like, maybe that happens? You're into someone and everyone else just…isn't them."

Was White talking about him? Damn, that would be nice. Ryan had acted like Braxton shouldn't make a big deal about sex. Maybe he was right. And maybe Braxton was finally getting an opportunity to see that what they'd have wasn't a big deal. Ryan clearly saw it as nothing.

Him as nothing.

Just a warm body. And White was warm and close and just as drunk and confused as he was.

"But you don't have to be into someone for them to get you off?" Braxton turned on his side and stared at the man beside him. A bit blurry, but he saw no judgment in his eyes. "I don't want to play with girls. I'm tired of pretending I do."

"Then stop."

"I want to stop. But…I've jerked off thinking of Hunt. And that was good, but nothing compared to fucking the one man I really want." Braxton slid his hand over White's chest, jerking away when he abruptly sat up. "I'm sorry. I don't mean I want you—"

"Okay, that's good." White rubbed a hand over his face. "Because you're not fucking me, kid."

That White didn't move away was a bit confusing. He didn't stop Braxton from touching him again. His breaths quickened and he eased back against the pillows as Braxton's fingers drifted down to his stomach.

"I don't want to fuck you, White." Braxton slid his hand over White's rock hard cock. He was being way too bold. He needed to make sure there weren't any misunderstandings. "But I want to suck your dick. I want to know I can do that without it meaning anything."

"Fuck." White's hips rose as Braxton continued to stroke him through his pants. "I wanna let you."

"Why?"

"Because it not meaning anything sounds good. And that feels good. Maybe that's all that matters. Maybe I'll stop thinking so much if I just take what I can get."

Then we're on the exact same page.

Braxton moved slowly, unzipping White's pants and sliding down, groaning as White's fingers tangled in his hair. Sex didn't have to mean anything. He could make another man feel good. He wanted to. This was the first time since Ryan that he hadn't felt like he was being smothered. White's dick on his tongue was hot. Thick. The bit of precum on the tip made his mouth water.

Then White went soft. Braxton tried moving faster, tried letting his hand move with his lips with a bit of pressure from both, but White stopped him, cupping his cheek.

His words were slurred, but they got through to Braxton.

He wanted to get more food. Call that girl and her friends.

A knock at the door got him moving. Were the girls there already? That was fast. Maybe someone was here to complain about the music. He'd hardly noticed, but it was a bit loud. He opened the door, his face heating as the girls filled the room.

They smelled nice, but he knew what them being here meant. The same thing it did when he was with Hunt and there were girls and he had to play his part.

At least the girls knew what they wanted. There was no conversation. No confusion. He let one of the girls take off his clothes. His vision was so blurred he couldn't even make out her face, but he heard the condom wrapper. Brushed her hand away and led her to White.

White wanted this.

He didn't.

But he didn't stop the second girl from dropping to her knees and sucking his dick. He focused on White as the man went down on one girl, while fucking another. The muscles of his ass moved rhythmically and Braxton couldn't look away. The pressure on his dick felt good. He could do this. Get on that bed with White and enjoy himself in the heat and slick slide of skin on skin, feeding on the other man's pleasure.

Pleasure he couldn't give him, but did that matter anymore?

Another knock and he eased away from the girls. Grabbed a towel at the last minute to cover himself. Turned off the music which was way too loud.

He opened the door and tried to stand straight as Vanek stared at him. A few feet behind him, Pisch froze.

I don't know what I did, but it was bad. I shouldn't be here.

This was his room.

You're fucked up and now everyone knows it.

He had to calm down. No one knew anything. Maybe they were here because they were bored.

"Hey, Vanek. Pischlar." He gave them a jerky nod. "Umm...what's up?"

Vanek moved away from the door. "Coach is looking for you. You might want to just call him though because you smell like a fucking brewery. You're lucky we ain't playing tomorrow."

I do? Shit, this wasn't good. But he was too gone to care too much. "Yeah, I—"

"Get your ass back in here, Braxton!" White shouted. The music came back on.

Braxton smiled at Vanek, hoping the man heard the apology in his tone. He couldn't explain what was happening. And didn't really want to. "I'll call him. Thanks for the message."

Vanek and Pisch weren't here for fun. They would judge him and he couldn't deal with that. Not when he was already judging himself. He pushed the door shut and his racing mind went quiet.

Pretend everything is fine. White didn't want you alone, but he wants you with him now.

That had to be enough, because he couldn't have better.

He'd done this before. Played the part and things turned out okay. He just had to forget that one night when things were real. When he'd been able to be himself.

That wasn't today. It wouldn't be tomorrow. But right now… did that even matter?

White was hiding too. Braxton knew he was. The man probably wouldn't look so blissed out if he'd known Pischlar knew what he was doing. But, for whatever reason, White was okay with what he could have. These women who expected nothing. A night with some pleasure.

Wanting more hurt, and Braxton didn't want to hurt anymore.

Tonight, he didn't have to.

CHAPTER 9

Life had been kicking Ryan's ass for a while now and he needed a damn break. At least his sister was doing better, and whatever had gone down in her relationship—he didn't get many details and wouldn't ask, Laura was comfortable talking to him, but not about private matters between her and her Domme—seemed to have worked itself out. She was happy, back at work, and starting to turn her focus on how out of it he'd been.

As much as he loved her, he couldn't tell her. Not when he didn't really understand it himself. A dozen times over the past few months he'd been tempted to call Braxton, but he always talked himself out of it. Giving the kid false hope would be cruel.

The young man had pushed the boundaries the last time Ryan even considered giving him another chance.

But damn it, he'd fucked up Ryan's ability to enjoy anyone else.

Every twink at the club that he'd once enjoyed reminded him of Braxton. Only, he kept his sessions short, made sure the eager submissives enjoyed themselves, then…ended things without claiming any satisfaction for himself. For a man who'd once had a very healthy sexual drive, his lack of interest was getting out of hand.

Just call him. Stop worrying about what he might want in the future. You don't even know what you want now.

Very true, but that concerned him as well. Since when was he this indecisive?

Taking a look at the time on his phone he sighed and pushed off the couch. He had a few days off—and no say about it because the captain was worried he'd get himself shot with how many hours he was putting in and how tired he always was. Might as well put that time to good use and figure out what to do with the boy who'd gotten his hooks in him.

Calling past midnight might give the wrong impression, but showing up at the club where they'd first met and seeing if he was there? Good neutral territory. He'd have the option of making whatever happened a casual hookup or…maybe more.

I'll know once I get there.

Less than twenty minutes later, he was regretting leaving the damn house. He ordered a beer from a waiter he didn't recognize, taking a sip and hardly tasting it, his eyes never leaving the stage. As always, there were performers up there. Moving to the music, enticing the crowd.

Usually an enjoyable show to watch.

Except one of those men belonged to him.

Don't even go there. You cut him loose.

Perhaps, but he'd done it for the boy's own good, not to have him do whatever the fuck he was doing now. Stripping on stage? Damn it, Braxton was a professional hockey player. He was risking his career and for what? Was he that desperate for attention?

The little black mask he was wearing wouldn't save him if anyone figured out who he was. The urge to storm onto the stage and drag him off became more than misplaced possessiveness. Someone needed to protect the boy from his own foolishness.

But when he caught Braxton's gaze on him, he realized this wasn't a young man simply being a little wild. Braxton began to move more provocatively. As though to tempt Ryan. As though to test his reactions.

How often had he come here and done this, hoping Ryan would show up? Couldn't have been too often, Ryan would've heard something from his friends who worked here. Unless... Braxton wasn't stupid. Terry or Gordon would've dragged him off the stage by his ear. The owner, however, probably enjoyed the additional eye candy.

Either way, if he was reading the situation right, Braxton was using this to get Ryan's attention. He couldn't encourage that. If he left now, hopefully Braxton would see his ridiculous plan was ineffective and maybe then they could have a real conversation.

He couldn't make himself move though.

Part of him felt responsible for this. Granted, he hadn't approved of Braxton's pushy attempts to contact him before, but this was a whole different level. If the boy was his sub he'd—

But he's not.

Not yet.

Ryan ground his teeth, taking another gulp of beer and considering his options. He could always speak to the owner and have Braxton barred from the club, but letting the man know he was interested in Braxton wasn't ideal either. He liked his privacy and that kind of drama went against his every instinct. It could also put Braxton in danger. Some of Ryan's high profile arrests had connections who'd pay good money to learn about any weaknesses Ryan might have.

Like it or not, Braxton had quickly become one of them. He'd never forgive himself if the boy became a target because of him.

Which made the idea of seeing him again seem even worse, but now that he had, he couldn't completely abandon the idea.

Movement from the edge of the stage caught his eye. He recognized two of the players from Braxton's team, neither looking too thrilled. Another gulp of beer and Ryan caught Braxton's eyes again. His muscles tensed as Braxton dropped to his knees, drawing cheers and whistles from the crowd. He was a damn good dancer. Fucking sexy as hell up there. From the gleam in his eyes between the slits of the mask, Ryan could tell Braxton had shut out everyone except Ryan. As though he was dancing for him alone.

Ryan rubbed a hand over his face, finished his beer, then stood.

For both their sakes, he had to ignore the temptation in those eyes. If he didn't, he'd resent his hand being forced in such a reckless way. He'd have more reasons to convince himself keeping his distance was the smartest choice.

He'd see Braxton again. On his terms.

That in mind, he turned and walked out of the club without looking back. But at the sound of a fist hitting flesh, he smiled.

His boy had good friends. They'd take care of him.

At least until Ryan claimed that responsibility. Then Braxton's safety, and his discipline, would be up to him.

Looks like you've made up your mind about what to do with him then, Hamilton.

He let out a soft laugh and shook his head as he hit the street and headed to his car.

Looks like.

CHAPTER 10

Ever since that morning with Pischlar, Braxton had been...off. He'd been enjoying the freedom of not giving a fuck about sex and who he fooled around with, but when he'd heard that door slam he knew he'd gone too far. Maybe it wasn't hurting him, he'd shut himself off from being emotionally attached to anyone, but White was his friend.

White had fun fucking you.

Braxton slumped back on his bed and put his hands over his face. He wasn't a complete fool, he'd figured out that White only played along after rescuing Braxton from his own stupidity because Pischlar was there. And White was in love with Pischlar.

He just hadn't accepted it yet.

And Braxton had just made things so much more difficult for them both, simply by being there. By being the type of toy Pischlar liked playing with, while White was still confused and incapable of being that detached.

He really hoped they'd work it out and not end up like him, still trying to get noticed by the man who'd tossed him aside months ago. How pathetic could Braxton be? Why couldn't he just forget about Ryan? Why couldn't he keep being as carefree as Pischlar?

Not that Pischlar's attitude was working out for him. He'd been uncharacteristically quiet after White left. Still kind to Braxton, but there was no mistaking the subtle hints that he wanted him to leave. Days later and things still felt unsettled. The team needed Braxton to give his all, and he was, but off the ice the rest of his life was…on hold.

But maybe it didn't have to be anymore. Ryan's reaction had made things clearer than ever. He'd walked out. He didn't care.

There was no point in chasing after that dream of who Ryan was anymore. He wasn't interested. He'd never be interested. It would be best to leave him as a sweet memory, Braxton's first real lover, his first connection.

His first heartbreak.

Rolling his eyes at that, Braxton sat up, then pushed off the bed. He was being pathetic. He'd been pathetic for a while, even though he'd made the effort to explore his options. If he'd fooled around with someone other than White, things wouldn't have gotten so messed up.

His first clue should've been "I'm straight…I think."

No more boys who were questioning. And sure as hell no more girls. That wasn't fair to anyone.

He might not be ready to come out publicly, but he knew what he wanted, and it wasn't to play a role anymore. He also couldn't be acting out and getting on stage, or he'd lose the one thing he was sure of in his life.

His career.

But he was freaking restless and lonely and he couldn't just mope around his apartment. He strode across his room, glancing in the mirror as he passed and making a face. He was a mess. His shirt and jeans looked slept in. Because they had been. If he had a game today he'd shower and shave and pull himself together, but the team was on a rare long stretch between games. Four days, two without even practice because Coach wanted them to rest up after their last road trip.

So whatever. He'd go out like this, keep his head down under a random ball cap, and grab a beer somewhere local. Maybe a few beers. He needed to find a way to unwind.

Two hours later and a couple of drinks in and he wasn't feeling any better. His problems hadn't gone away, he'd simply found a new location to try to avoid them in. And was failing.

By his side a stool was dragged out. There was a heavy sigh.

He stiffened, lifting his head slowly.

Ryan stared back at him, lips slanted with amusement as Braxton jumped back and almost fell over. He put a steadying hand on Braxton's arm and clucked his tongue. "All that effort to get my attention and you try to run the second you have it?"

Lips parted, Braxton quickly shook his head. "I'm not. I—what are you doing here?"

"I was heading to your place to talk to you and saw you come in." Ryan lowered his hand and sat back, his smile fading. "We need to talk, but I wanted an idea of where your head was at first. Have you been drinking a lot?"

Pressing his eyes shut, Braxton groaned. The man had hunted him down for a lecture? Fun. He shook his head. "No, I usually don't drink at all—I don't want it to fuck up my play. But now and then when I get time off." With a shrug he opened his eyes, refusing to let Ryan make him feel ashamed of living his own damn life. "If that's what you wanted to talk about, don't worry. I'm Gucci."

Brow furrowed, Ryan looked confused for a moment. Then he chuckled. "Sometimes I forget how young you are."

Braxton began to rise. "Oh fuck off, not that again."

One hard look from Ryan stilled him. "If you walk away from me now, Braxton, we're done. You've been pushing me in every way possible. In ways I shouldn't tolerate. And will not going forward." Ryan leaned closer, his voice taking on a dark edge. "What happened on that stage? What exactly were you trying to accomplish?"

"I wanted you to talk to me. To admit there's something between us." Braxton's jaw ticked as he recalled the moment he'd decided he was wasting his time. "You left."

"Yes. I did." Ryan's tone didn't change. "I won't be manipulated and I saw your friends were there to save you."

"That and more."

The reaction Braxton got wasn't what he'd expected. Ryan had spent so much time trying to prove he wasn't interested. That they had nothing. And never would. But his expression didn't match that at all. There was shock. Then rage. He was grinding his teeth and fisting his hand on the bar like he wanted to hit something.

Staring straight ahead, Ryan motioned to the bartender and ordered a whiskey on the rocks. Once he was served he took a long gulp. Nodded to himself. "They took advantage of you?"

"What? No, Pisch and White would never do that." Braxton grabbed Ryan's wrist. "Don't even think that. You said I was young and I shouldn't take sex too seriously. So I stopped."

"You...stopped?"

"Yeah, I sucked White's dick. It didn't go well, so he invited some girls in and..." Braxton swallowed when Ryan turned to him and arched a brow. "And I can't keep doing that. I don't want to. Pisch is easy. Hell, it's what everyone calls him. Letting him and White fuck me was like...better. For a bit, things were better."

Groaning, Ryan rubbed a hand over his face. "'For a bit'?"

"They're... It's complicated. Not my story to tell, man." Braxton began picking the label off his beer bottle, not really in the mood to drink anymore. "I like you, Ryan. A lot. But I get that you don't feel the same and I'll get over it. It just took some time to realize I was being an idiot."

"You weren't the only one." Ryan held up one hand before Braxton could interrupt. "You've pushed every boundary I have and even after I agreed to talk to you, you were impatient and caught me at the worst time. But I also realized you couldn't possibly know that. I could've sent you a text and let you know I was busy. I was worried about leading you on and I wanted to avoid...complications."

"I can see why now." Braxton ducked his head and snickered when Ryan gave him a level look. He didn't seem to like reminders of what had happened with White and Pisch, which was funny, considering Ryan had told him to go out and experience things. "Hey, are you..." His eyes went wide. "You're jealous, aren't you?"

"Don't be ridiculous. You giving a friend a bad blowjob before having horrible sex with a bunch of random—"

"Pischlar made sure the next blowjob was much better." Braxton's lips slanted. "I seem to do better with instructions."

For a long time, Ryan didn't say anything. He turned his focus back to his drink, swigging it, then ordering another. He inhaled slowly, shaking his head, as though having a silent conversation with himself.

"Pischlar's a Dom." Ryan's voice was quiet. Controlled. "White seems rather submissive. And you definitely are. I can see how you'd enjoy a scenario that would involve you surrendering control. But you won't be doing it with Pischlar again."

Braxton rubbed his thighs, confused. "Yes, I know. This has already been established because—"

"Do you still want to explore what's between us, Braxton?"

The way Ryan asked made Braxton hesitate. He wasn't asking him out on a date. He wasn't being sweet and romantic—not that Braxton really expected that.

Or expected anything.

He had a feeling 'exploring' anything with Ryan, anything beyond one night, would be intense. The idea thrilled him and scared him all at once. Ryan mentioned Pischlar being a Dom like it was a familiar thing. An everyday, normal part of life. His life.

"I do, but…you're a Dom too, aren't you?"

Nodding slowly, Ryan met and held his gaze. "I am. And I'm not interested in a partner who isn't in the lifestyle. I don't date casually—or at all, to be perfectly honest. I fucked who I wanted when I didn't have time to commit to a full scene, and went to the local BDSM club to satisfy my other needs. Obviously I wouldn't do that if I was in a relationship."

Oh…

Oh!

All right, this was starting to make more sense. Ryan worked a lot, and from the little Braxton knew of those on the team in BDSM relationships, it took time and trust, neither of which Ryan would have with him after one night. And he hadn't wanted to try to build it. Not when he could keep things simple.

Braxton had been asking him for something much more… complicated. More than he'd ever considered. He hadn't understood why Ryan wanted to end things. Why he wouldn't want to be with Braxton again when things had been so good between them.

I guess asking someone to be your submissive isn't a "Let's grab a coffee," kinda chat.

But they were here now. Having that conversation. The very one Braxton had been wanting for so long.

"Yes, I still want this, Ryan."

The edge of Ryan's lips quirked. "Are you sure?"

Braxton frowned. "Don't I sound it?"

"You do, but you have no clue what you're in for." He put his arm on the backrest of Braxton's stool, coming closer to whisper in his ear. "This won't be just you on your knees, holding still so I can fuck your mouth. This won't be Pisch giving you a few playful commands. You will be mine in every way. So I'll ask you again." Ryan's lips brushed his ear. "Are you sure?"

Heat flowed in a steady pulse from the base of Braxton's spine, right into his swelling dick. Ryan's breath had a shiver of anticipation skittering across his flesh. A contrast of hot and cold, eagerness with an edge of fear, all wrapped up in temptation.

His mouth went dry, but he managed a single word. "Yes."

Ryan eased away and inclined his head. "Very well. I've looked at your schedule. You have practice in two days. I won't do anything to hamper your performance, but I'll take that time to see if this is worth either of us ignoring all the reasons we shouldn't be together."

"Yeah?" Braxton let out a nervous laugh. "Because I can't think of a single one."

That seemed to amuse Ryan, but he simply lifted his shoulders. "Come then. I owe you a punishment for what you pulled at the club. You'll be lucky if I ever allow you to return."

Blinking at Ryan, Braxton tried to wrap his mind around what he'd just said. "A punishment? But…you weren't my Dom yet."

"You were trying to get my attention. You have it. We've discussed this already."

That didn't sound fair, but Braxton had a feeling this was a test. His lips thinned. "As far as I know, these things are negotiated first. Let's do that."

Ryan's eyes warmed. "Agreed."

"Just like that?"

The man laughed, dropping a few bills on the bar to pay for their drinks, then nodding toward the exit. "Yes. I need to know you'll be able to communicate with me. If your crush on me prevented you from doing so, I'd be dropping you off at home and continuing with my day. Maybe try this again when you grow up a bit."

Face heating, Braxton shoved his hands in his pockets, following Ryan to his car. "This isn't a crush."

"Noted."

"And I know all about punishments. And 'funishments'. I'm fine with either, within reason." He got into the passenger side, hands fisted on his thighs as Ryan got in behind the wheel. "All I ask is that you let me know what I did wrong, so I can do better next time." He thought of the club, of being up on that stage and…he wished Ryan had been his Dom then. That he'd come onto the stage and showed he gave a damn. Brought Braxton home and made it even more clear. His eyes burned when he considered what had happened instead. He'd had fun with Pisch and White, but to them he'd just done something stupid and he wouldn't ever again.

Reaching out, Ryan put his hand on Braxton's cheek with a light pressure until he turned to face him. "What was that thought?"

Pressing his tongue into his bottom lip, Braxton stared into Ryan's eyes, his own burning as Ryan somehow forced him to face his own feelings with nothing but a calm look. "That night was really bad for me. Not the stuff after, that was fun, but also… shallow. I wish…I wish there was a way to make that feeling go away."

"You need closure. You need to face that what you did wasn't okay, for either of us." Ryan's framed Braxton's jaw with his hand. "I think a punishment will do that, but you're right. I wasn't your Dom. You hadn't given me that control yet. You still haven't."

"I want to."

"Then I'll take it." Ryan brushed his lips over Braxton's, a light, soothing kiss that eased away the uncertainty, while still making Braxton want to cry.

He wasn't even sure why. His emotions were suddenly all over the place. He blinked fast as Ryan drew away from him and started the car. No way was he going to break down. The man wasn't sure if he could take this and falling apart now would only show him he was right.

Ryan shot him a concerned glance when he straightened and rubbed his hands over his face. Then his expression hardened. "It's like that, is it? You've been shutting off your feelings more and more since that night with me. And that's my fault."

"No it's not, you weren't—"

"Your boyfriend or your Dom. But for the next two days, I am. And if nothing else, I'll help you regain that confidence you had. I'll make it so you aren't afraid to cry."

Sniffling a little, Braxton laughed. "I'm not spending the next two days crying. That won't convince you to keep me."

"Don't be so sure about that."

This had to be the weirdest conversation he'd ever had with anyone. But he could tell Ryan wasn't joking. His breath caught as he realized he'd just hopped in the car of a man he hardly knew and agreed to give up control for the next two days.

He should be very afraid. Ryan didn't sound like he planned to make this easy.

And for some reason, that excited Braxton even more.

CHAPTER 11

Like the last time Braxton had been here, he noticed Ryan surveying the area for any threat. Not as though he was really worried, more out of habit. Unlike last time though, there wasn't the same sense of urgency coming from the other man. Braxton wanted there to be, he wanted to be pulled past the front door and fucked on the closest hard surface.

Instead, he followed Ryan in, chewing on his bottom lip and watching as he took off his shoes. Was this part of the punishment they'd talked about? Was Ryan gonna give him the silent treatment?

Once he'd straightened, Ryan turned to face him, arms folded over his chest. His lips quirked slightly as he watched Braxton fidget. "No need to be nervous, boy. You can end all this with a word."

"I don't want to end anything." Braxton hiked up his chin. "And I'm not nervous, I just want to know what the fuck you plan—"

Ryan's expression hardened and Braxton decided now would be a very good time to stop talking. He swallowed hard even as the blood began to pulse into his dick. All right, maybe he was a bit nervous. The man was scary with that look in his eyes and for some reason it was damn hot.

But Braxton didn't want to piss him off. He didn't want Ryan to regret giving him the next two days, after he'd been determined to give him nothing. They had amazing chemistry. Braxton wanted to be the man who Ryan wanted at the end of a rough day. The man Ryan got everything he needed from.

He just had no clue where to start.

Moving closer to him, Ryan stroked his cheek and lightly clucked his tongue. "Braxton, stop trying to anticipate what I want from you. You're exactly where you wanted to be." He tipped Braxton's chin up with a finger, kissing him with a gentle press of his lips, sliding his tongue into his mouth, every movement so slow it put Braxton in a zone where nothing needed to be rushed.

His kiss was telling Braxton not to worry. Telling him these two days were the beginning of something amazing.

But the kiss was over much too soon and Braxton groaned as Ryan backed away from him. Lips still parted, desperate for more, Braxton struggled not to pout when Ryan gave him one of his amused smiles. The man knew exactly what he was doing. This was probably some kind of test.

No way would Braxton fail the first one, so he remained in place as Ryan's gaze drifted over him.

"When you're in my home, there will be some basic rules for you to follow. Since you're new at being a submissive, we'll keep things simple." Ryan smiled at Braxton's nod. "You're to remove your clothing at the door, fold them neatly, then bring them to me. Unless instructed otherwise, you'll kneel by my side when I'm sitting and wait to be acknowledged. You may speak whenever you'd like, but it will be done respectfully and you will call me 'Sir'. Understood?"

This was really happening. Braxton inhaled roughly, his erection giving a painful throb as he nodded. He shouldn't be this needy, not when he'd been fucked so recently, but they hadn't been Ryan. Ryan somehow managed to get him all worked up without much effort and it had Braxton anticipating his next move.

Which he wasn't supposed to do.

Hooking his fingers at the bottom of his shirt, he quickly pulled it off, then kicked off his sneakers and undid his jeans. His cheeks heated as he remembered he'd slept in these clothes. If he'd known he was going to see Ryan he'd have showered and shaved and worn something nice to impress him. He ducked his head as he sensed Ryan's eyes on him while he folded the clothes which should probably get thrown in the nearest hamper.

At least he'd been relaxing lately and not working out. If he stank, he'd be absolutely humiliated.

Steady footsteps moving away from him brought his head up and he watched as Ryan walked down the short hall, disappearing into a room without a door. He followed quietly, his heart pounding as he stepped into the living room, standing there awkwardly as Ryan turned on the TV.

If this was part of the test, it was easy enough. He went to Ryan, laid his pile of clothes on the sofa beside him, then knelt on the soft, round, dark grey area rug. He wasn't sure if he should face the TV or Ryan, but guessed it would be kinda weird if he knelt there, staring at the guy, so he chose the former.

After a moment Ryan reached out and pressed Braxton's head against his knee, then began stroking his hair. The tension eased out of Braxton's shoulders and he relaxed, his eyes drifting shut as he settled in for however long Ryan wanted him to be here, just like this. There was something soothing about the whole experience. No pressure, no wondering if he was doing the right thing. He was doing what he'd been asked. Nothing more, nothing less.

"Much better." Ryan leaned forward once whatever news show he'd been watching was finished, lips curving as Braxton blinked up at him. "You seem much more comfortable."

"I am. I mean, not that I was uncomfortable before...exactly." Braxton frowned when Ryan arched a brow at him. Oh yeah. "Umm, Sir. I'm comfortable with you, but I know if I fuck up I could go months without seeing you again. Or never see you."

"Hmm, yes, I can see how that would add a lot of pressure. Which isn't what I want for you." Ryan stroked Braxton's hair again. "The next two days is to see if this is something both of us will enjoy, Braxton. I'm tempted to tell you I refuse to let anyone else ever touch you again. That you're mine from here on. But I'd be reacting out of jealousy and a possessiveness I haven't earned. You may end up deciding I'm too overbearing and boring. That this kind of life isn't for you."

Braxton's lips parted. He wanted to argue, but part of him was stunned Ryan had admitted all that.

No hesitation. Complete honesty.

He couldn't give the man any less. "The last thing you'd ever be to me is boring, but I get it. I haven't ever wanted a relationship—the ones I thought I should want never felt right. But I'm a hockey player and you might not want to put up with me being gone all the time and being full of energy and eating a lot and being..." Okay, maybe this was too much honesty? Ryan looked ready to laugh as Braxton tried to figure out all the negative things about himself. "Being way too chatty."

"You do tend to rush out words, but it doesn't bother me. You're also capable of having an intelligent conversation. And you're passionate about everything. I like that." Ryan leaned forward and kissed him, letting out a laugh against his lips. "But you smell like the inside of my gym bag and it's rather distracting. Come, I think it's time I show you how I enjoy caring for my pet."

Cheeks heating, Braxton stood as Ryan did. "Sorry, I didn't think I was that bad. I took a shower yesterday, but I kinda bummed around the house and slept in my clothes."

"I figured it was something like that. If it's any consolation, my gym bag doesn't smell anything like yours probably does. I keep what belongs to me very clean." Ryan slid his hand around the back of Braxton's neck. "Unless I choose to get it messy. I haven't decided which way I want you right now. Maybe a little of both?"

How that could be accomplished, Braxton had no idea. But the firm grip on the back of his neck and the lust in Ryan's eyes had him eager to find out.

Like the rest of Ryan's house, the area at the top of the stairs was all in natural, masculine colors. He barely remembered anything but the bedroom since they'd spent most of their one night in there. He'd been on a sex high when he'd used the bathroom, but it was pretty standard. Big, clawfoot bath with a separate glass shower a few feet away, dark blue tiles, a plain sink with a small counter, a wicker hamper, and a rack above the toilet with necessities and thick, white towels.

The room smelled nice, a bit like some fresh kind of light scented cleaner and the fabric softener used on the towels. Braxton did his own laundry and cleaning, but his stuff never smelled this good. Always like harsh cleaners, plain laundry soap —even though his mom had gotten on his back to take the extra steps to make his clothes nice and soft. He'd never really cared before, but now he wished he was up to Ryan's standards.

"You're staring at my towels." Ryan stepped up behind him, laughter in his tone as he pressed his lips to Braxton's bare shoulder. "Please tell me you own some?"

"Of course I do. They're just all worn out and stiff."

"I'm sure they do the job." Ryan stepped past him, leaning into the shower to turn on the spray. "If you ever do laundry here, I'll show you what I expect."

Braxton cocked his head. "That's something you'd want me to do for you?"

"Mhmm, if service is part of submission that you enjoy. Or if you're here often enough that you'll need to do your share." He chuckled when Braxton stared at him. "We are not spending the next two days with you fixated on there being a time limit. You're not the only one who hopes this works out. I decided I wanted more time with you. I won't be setting you up to fail."

"But it's still a test."

Ryan inclined his head. "Yes. And so far, you're doing well. Now get in."

At first Braxton couldn't meet Ryan's eyes as he stepped into the shower. Was the man just gonna watch him wash to make sure he did a good job? He must be so fucking disgusted that—

His throat tightened as Ryan unbuttoned his shirt and hung it up behind the door. The air seemed to leave the room as Ryan undid his belt. Pulled off his pants and laid them on the counter. Fuck, the man was incredible. Every hard muscle, every inch of smooth skin, slightly more tanned than the last time they'd been together as though he'd spent a lot of time in the sun. Even the light hair on his chest and his thighs seemed to be a bit lighter, as though the sun had given a golden hue to the dark brown hair, though that was probably just the lighting in the bathroom.

When Ryan stepped into the shower, Braxton licked his lips, moving deeper under the spray to give him more room. His gaze dropped to Ryan's dick, nice and thick and already half erect. He wanted to get on his knees and slide his lips over it, but first he needed to know what Ryan wanted from him.

"Fuck, I love it when you look at me like that." Ryan reached up and smoothed Braxton's hair back from his face. "I'm going to enjoy you tonight, but there's still a punishment to get out of the way, yes?"

Chewing on his bottom lip, Braxton nodded. He'd managed to push that aside with how easy Ryan had made everything, but it would be hanging between them until it was done. And this was something he'd asked for. Sure, Ryan had mentioned it, but more like he needed to know what Braxton would be comfortable with and make sure he wouldn't blindly go along with every suggestion.

He wouldn't, but Ryan agreeing to punish him was…was a way to show he cared.

"We're still learning much about one another, Braxton, and even punishments shouldn't go beyond your limits. There are two kinds that I'll usually stick to. Spanking and isolation." Ryan's brow furrowed. "I don't think isolation would be good for you in this instance, but I don't know if you're ready to be spanked."

If anyone else was saying that, Braxton would've laughed it off. But Ryan was serious and he didn't think this would be the playful kind of spanking.

He also didn't think it was a coincidence Ryan had brought it up when they were both in the shower.

Swallowing hard, he met Ryan's eyes. "Here?"

Ryan inclined his head. "It will hurt more, but the effects won't last. Except in the way they're meant to."

That doesn't sound like much fun. Braxton took a deep breath. "But when you're done, it's over, right? You won't be mad anymore?"

"Damn it, pet." Ryan pulled him close, delving his fingers into his hair and kissing him in a way that was so tender Braxton's eyes teared. "I'm not mad at you now. You worried me, but it wasn't my place to protect you. I'm hoping it will be now."

"I'm sorry."

"I know." Ryan shook his head. "I won't enjoy this, Braxton. And if you tell me you've changed your mind, I'll accept that."

Braxton believed him, but it didn't matter. The dynamics between them were becoming something he craved and he didn't think Ryan truly saw that yet. This would put what he'd done behind them and prove he was ready for the kind of relationship Ryan wanted. Prove that Braxton wanted the same thing.

"I haven't changed my mind."

Nodding slowly, Ryan brought their lips together one last time before stepping back and squaring his shoulders. "Hands against the wall then, and brace your feet apart in a position you feel secure in. We'll go with ten this time. Keep things light."

Following Ryan's instructions, Braxton lowered his head between his arms. Braced for the first impact.

Instead, Ryan ran his hand over Braxton's ass, as though to make sure he was prepared. He spoke softly. "Count for me."

The first strike made Braxton's knees buckle and he bit into his cheek to keep from crying out. He wasn't sure what Ryan's idea of 'keeping things light' was, but they clearly weren't on the same page. Not that he minded, even though he fought the automatic instinct to swear at the man.

Ryan was a Dom. And he was taking Braxton seriously as a sub.

This was good.

Fucking hurt, but…still good.

"One."

Another smack, this one echoing through the room, the sting spreading over Braxton's flesh. He let out a rough sound in the back of his throat.

"Two."

The next five were just as hard, but he'd adjusted to the pain. He kept counting, hissing in air through his teeth, proud of how steady he was holding through the whole ordeal.

But then Ryan stopped.

Repositioned himself. And slapped Braxton's thigh.

This time, Braxton couldn't stop the sharp cry. Or the tears that filled his eyes. Damn it, why had he been so stupid? He'd thought Ryan walked away when he was on that stage because he didn't give a fuck, but instead he'd been concerned and forced to let Pischlar and White step in. If he'd tried to drag Braxton off that stage that night, where would they be now?

"Ei…eight."

Probably not, because Ryan would feel pressured and he'd have been pissed. Because Braxton had acted like a bratty kid who hadn't gotten his own way.

A slap on the other thigh. His legs shook and he sobbed. "Nine."

"Shh, you're doing so good, baby." Ryan rubbed away the sting. "I'm so fucking proud of you. One more. One more and then you're going to promise me I never have to do this again."

The gentle words made it hard not to break down in tears, but Braxton simply nodded. The last slap, right on the center of his ass, hurt, but something had changed. He trembled as he tried to voice the final number. Tears joined the water from the shower, spilling down his cheeks. Ryan's hands were on him again and his quiet words were like a balm on the regret and pain and confusion.

"Say it, pet. You're done. You're done and you did very well. Stand up straight and look at me."

Straightening, Braxton turned, feeling kinda pathetic, all teary and sniffling. But the way Ryan was looking at him made it all worth it. "Ten?"

"Yes." Ryan's lips curved. "How do you feel?"

"I…" Braxton sniffed. Then burst out in tears. Fuck, Ryan was going to send him home. He was gonna think he couldn't handle this. But he could. Crying kinda felt good, like all the pressure inside was releasing, but that didn't make any sense.

He told Ryan as much, between hiccupping sobs even as he tried to contain himself.

And Ryan hugged him. Which was…amazing. He hugged him and kissed his hair. "It makes sense, Braxton. You were trying to be someone you're not, and prove you didn't care what happened to you. Which was hurting you."

"If White and Pischlar hadn't been there that night…"

"I know." Ryan put his hands on Braxton's shoulders and gently eased him back. "Then again, if I hadn't seen them, I wouldn't have left. But you made your decisions and I made mine. We're moving past it now."

"Except now you know I'll start crying over stupid shit."

Ryan gave him a stern look. "No, now I know you feel safe crying in front of me. That's not a bad thing."

All right, he could see how that would be good. If he was gonna be Ryan's submissive, this probably wouldn't be the first time he cried in front of him, though he hoped it didn't happen too often. He wanted Ryan happy with him.

"Crying good. Stripping for strangers, bad." Braxton ticked each off on his fingers, continuing when Ryan's lips quirked. "Calling you at work, bad. Losing my bike…bad."

With an abrupt laugh, Ryan shoved him back under the shower spray. "You're ridiculous. Behave while I clean you. You've had all the pain I intend to give you tonight."

"How would you cleaning me hurt?"

Lips slanting, Ryan reached over and picked up a package of fresh razors from a shelf and took one out. After setting the rest aside and grabbing a can of shaving cream, he nudged Braxton against the wall away from the shower now. "It will only hurt if you distract me."

"Oh fuck."

"Mhmm." Ryan chuckled as he took a knee. He filled his palm with shaving cream, then eyed Braxton, leaning forward and sliding his lips over Braxton's dick. He took him in deep, swallowing around him. When Braxton cursed again, he drew away and began spreading the foam over his balls. "Do try to keep that out of my way. I wouldn't want to slip."

Jaw clenched, Braxton grabbed his dick, trying to decide if Ryan enjoyed messing with him, or if he was just plain evil. Having a razor brushing over his balls as Ryan held them taut made him think the latter. He pressed his eyes shut and tried to focus on Ryan touching him, rather than the blade moving over him. If his dick went soft it would be in the danger zone.

"You're good at following orders. I appreciate that." Ryan rinsed off the blade, then stood and drew Braxton under the water. "Tell me how that feels while I wash your hair."

Moving his hand over his balls, Braxton let out a soft moan. Fuck, they were sensitive. He moaned again as Ryan started working the shampoo into his hair, his fingertips gently massaging his scalp. This was always Braxton's favorite part of getting his hair cut. Having someone else washing his hair.

But the hairdresser doing it wasn't like Ryan. Standing there, naked, with Ryan so close was somehow more intimate than anything else they'd done.

Ball shaving aside.

"That feels fucking awesome. My balls feel awesome. Everything is awesome." Braxton groaned shamelessly as Ryan's fingers moved to the back of his neck. "You can spank me whenever you want if this is my reward."

Chuckling, Ryan made him turn and face him as he rinsed his hair. "This isn't a reward for the spanking. And since it clearly isn't a hard limit, I'll spank you whenever I please. You'll know when it's for a punishment. I won't take it so easy on you next time."

"Easy?" Braxton yelped as Ryan slapped his thigh, reminding him of the lingering ache there, which spread to the rest of his ass. "Yeah, I'm gonna shut up now."

"That would be wise." But Ryan seemed like he was having fun. He washed Braxton's body with a facecloth, then got out of the shower ahead of him, holding out a towel once he'd wrapped another around himself.

Turning off the shower, Braxton thanked Ryan, took the towel, and began drying his hair as Ryan motioned for him to follow him out of the bathroom. Despite the throbbing heat covering his ass, he really did feel awesome. As though the shower had cleaned him in every way. He got a fresh start with Ryan. He never thought he'd get one.

In Ryan's room, he waited by the door, not sure what he was supposed to do next. He pressed his teeth into his bottom lip as Ran sat on the edge of the bed.

Shit, the rules!

He dropped the towel and hurried to the bed, wincing as he dropped to his knees and the rough carpet scrapped them.

Sighing, Ryan shook his head. "We'll work on that."

Braxton ducked his head. "Sorry about that."

"Don't be, you're learning. But my submissive doesn't come to me like he's sliding into home base." Ryan ruffled his hair. "The only marks I want on you are the ones I've put there."

"Or I get on the ice."

"Yes, but do try to come home in one piece." For a second it looked like Ryan wanted to correct himself, but he simply laughed and shook his head. "Enough for one night. Get up here, I want to make sure I did a good job."

Pushing up to his feet, Braxton slid onto the bed without hesitation, but when Ryan eased him back and pressed his thighs apart, heat spilled from the back of his neck, up his ears and cheeks, and down to his chest. Fucking was one thing, but lying here, spread open, with Ryan's eyes on his dick was different. And only got worse when he cupped his ass cheeks and used his thumbs to completely expose his hole.

"Next time, I'll have you lying down like this so I can get everything." Ryan leaned down, flicking his tongue over the tight ring of muscle. He used his elbows to hold Braxton in place when his hips rose in response. "Be still, pet. I'm not finished inspecting you. This will be a regular thing I do. I like making sure you're ready for me."

He didn't think he could get any harder, but as Ryan teased him with the tip of his tongue, his pulsing dick pressed into his stomach and precum joined the droplets of water still glistening on his skin. He panted as Ryan's tongue pressed against him, reaching down to grab his hair, then stopping when Ryan looked up at him and his brow rose.

"Oh fuck. I don't know how long I can take this." Braxton reached up and hooked his fingers to the edge of the mattress. "Ryan…"

"Try again, pet." Ryan's tone held a hint of playful warning, but he continued to lick and press his tongue in a bit deeper.

Braxton grasped at the tantalizing burn that had his dick twitching and every muscle in his body tightening up. "Sir, please. I need…I need you to…"

Lifting his head, Ryan gave him a slow smile. He slid his fingers past his lips, slipping them out nice and slick with saliva. Then he brought the tips to Braxton's ass, holding his gaze. "This is what you'll get from me right now. And only this. If you can't come, we'll try again in the morning."

A whimper escaped Braxton as Ryan's fingers penetrated. He wasn't sure he could come without touching his dick. And he fucking needed to.

Rising up onto the bed, Ryan reclined on his side, his fingers deep inside Braxton, moving slowly. "You let White fuck you.

And Pischlar. Neither meant anything to you and you meant nothing to them, except as a friend willing to have a good time. You will give me more than that, Braxton." He curved his fingers, moving them in and out faster as Braxton's hips rose to meet them. "So much fucking more."

Braxton was close, but Ryan's words had him hovering on the edge, and he pressed his feet into the mattress, moving with Ryan, locked into the pressure and the sensation within. He was breathing like he'd taken double shifts on the ice during a penalty kill. Sweat was beading on his flesh. The precum on his dick was spilling steadily and it made his untouched dick even more sensitive.

"So fucking needy. Come for me, pet." Ryan whispered in his ear. "Come for me and I'll let you rest a bit before I fuck you. Before I fill you up with my come and leave you that way so I can take you again. Until all you can feel is the mess I've left of you." He withdrew his fingers. Spit on them again and brought them back, this time adding a third and using them all to stretch Braxton even more. "You won't be clean again until I decide to let you out of this bed. And I have you all to myself for two days."

"Oh God…God…" Braxton tipped his head back, muscles straining. "I'm close…"

"When you come I'll let you feel my mouth. I'll lick every last drop off of you. But you need to give it to me." Ryan sucked his earlobe into his mouth, biting hard enough to make it sting before letting out a rough sound. "Now."

The pressure, the curve of Ryan's fingers, the pain, all combined and overwhelmed Braxton's senses until he was crying out and jutting his hips up as the cum hit his stomach and his chest. He let out a shout as the intense pleasure barreled over him, stealing away his vision in a flash and leaving him breathless, all his strength leaving him as his dick gave one last jolt when Ryan bent down to lick it.

Like he'd promised, he cleaned every drop off of Braxton, withdrawing his fingers and rising up to give Braxton a deep, open mouthed kiss. His lips were slick and salty with Braxton's come and his dick was hard against Braxton's thigh, but he wasn't in a rush to continue. He even pulled Braxton's head onto his shoulder when his eyes started to drift shut.

Which didn't seem right. "Rya—Sir, I should—"

"Rest. As we discussed." Ryan pet his hair and made a soft, shushing sound. "You're physically and emotionally drained, Braxton. It's my job to take care of you while we're doing a scene. You need to learn to let me."

That sounded really nice. It still bothered Braxton that Ryan hadn't gotten off, but in this exchange, Ryan was the one in control. He'd take what he wanted when he thought Braxton was ready to give it.

And if what had happened was anything to go by?

Braxton would need his strength.

CHAPTER 12

Sleep had evaded Ryan so often over the past few months, feeling it calling as he held Braxton close confused the hell out of him. Until…

Until it didn't.

His life had consisted of dealing with one problem after another, worrying about his sister, taking on an overload of cases, dealing with the trouble the team got in while pretending he didn't give a damn about the Dartmouth Cobras. He'd avoided games and ignored avid fans because he didn't want to hear Braxton's name, even in passing.

Staying away from Braxton, denying his own feelings, had become a fulltime job. One he'd refused to quit for far too long. But, looking down at his sleeping face, Ryan couldn't remember why he'd been so fucking stubborn. Only that he was relieved to have finally stopped.

The light of dawn gleaming through the part in his curtains had him opening his eyes and he chuckled softly to himself, realizing he'd fallen asleep without meaning to. He'd had plans for Braxton last night, plans to wake him again and again, using him until the young man was sore and satisfied and understood how different things would be when they were together.

Would he still want this once he saw what was expected of him?

Ryan imagined he would. His new pet was eager to please and had plenty of stamina. If he was going to be in a relationship with a hockey player—of all things—he might as well enjoy the perks. And the challenges.

Such as, how long would it take to have Braxton begging him to stop? Would he ever, or would he take each and every bit of pleasure Ryan could give him, not needing any rest at all before Ryan proved this was only the beginning.

No better time than the present to find out.

Sliding his arm out from under Braxton's sleeping form, Ryan rose quietly and positioned the lube within easy reach, grabbing a condom to set close for when he needed it. Then he leaned over Braxton, drawing the sheet down to expose his naked body, brushing his lips over every bit of skin he exposed. Along his collarbone, over the smoothness of his chest, smiling when Braxton's nipples tightened before he'd even touched them.

He closed his mouth over one nipple, pressing down on Braxton's shoulder when he tried to turn to him, still half asleep. "Let's see how good you can be for me, pet."

"Mmmph." Braxton shifted his feet on the bed, moaning as he came fully awake when Ryan set his teeth into his nipple. "Good how?"

"For now, fold your hands behind your neck and let me take my time with you. No begging, no attempt to rush me. Take exactly what I offer and enjoy what I'm giving you."

Chewing on his bottom lip, Braxton nodded and positioned his hands. "Sounds easy enough."

Ryan smirked. *We shall see.*

Moving to Braxton's other nipple, Ryan traced around it with his tongue, then stopped to let the moisture cool. He blew on it lightly, enjoying Braxton's automatic shiver. Tiny goosebumps rose on Braxton's flesh as he flicked his tongue over the hard nub, then caught it between his teeth.

As he increased the pressure, Braxton squirmed.

"I haven't gotten nipple clamps in a while, but I believe I'll be getting some for you." Ryan pinched the nipple with his fingers as he returned to the first one, circling it with his tongue and using his breath to stimulate it before nipping it lightly, then harder as Braxton gasped and jerked his hips. "Would you like that?"

Breathing through parted lips, Braxton nodded. "I don't think there's much you could do to me that I wouldn't like."

Lips curving, Ryan began to kiss down the center of Braxton's chest. "There are things you may not be sure of, but I will test your limits. Many things you haven't even considered, or might find strange, would be an amazing experience for you."

A blush rose high on Braxton's cheeks as he watched Ryan move down his body. "Like what?"

Lifting his head, Ryan met Braxton's curious gaze and began idly stroking his fingers along the dip of Braxton's pelvis. "Bondage, edgeplay…maybe even sounding. The last will take a lot of training before I'm comfortable introducing you to something many consider extreme."

Braxton swallowed hard. "Do I wanna know what that is?"

Running his hand up and down Braxton's thigh, Ryan lifted his shoulders. "I don't know. Do you?"

Biting down on his lip even harder, Braxton nodded.

With a slow smile, Ryan curved his hand at the base of Braxton's dick, holding it lightly as Braxton began to pant. His struggle not to thrust himself into Ryan's hand was admirable.

"Sounding is when a long, thin rod is slowly inserted into the urethra." He loosely drew his hand up Braxton's cock and brushed his thumb over the bead of precum at the tip. "Done right it can reach the prostate and be quite…stimulating."

The color had left Braxton's cheeks, but his erection hadn't softened in the least. He was both terrified and aroused by the idea.

Perfect.

"That sounds really fucking dangerous." Braxton's lips moved silently for a moment. "What if you broke something?"

It was hard not to chuckle at that, but Ryan wouldn't laugh off Braxton's concerns. He rewarded the bare honesty of the question with another light stroke. "That kind of scene requires a great deal of trust. And knowledge on my part—though making sure you understand fully what is happening to you will help as well."

"Have you done it before?"

This time, when Ryan inclined his head, Braxton's dick began to soften. He didn't like the idea of Ryan with others, which Ryan could sympathize with. He wasn't exactly thrilled that Braxton had been letting his teammates fuck him.

He hadn't had a say in the matter before.

That had changed.

Bringing his lips down to kiss above where his hand was moving, he kept his voice low, using a soothing rhythm he knew would get Braxton to where he wanted him to be. "My experience will benefit you, pet. But I take commitments seriously and if we agree to one between us, there will be no one else. For either of us."

That brought a small smile to Braxton's lips. "Can we agree on that now?"

Ryan smiled back at him. "If you'd like, though you might change your mind when our two days are up."

Letting his eyes drift shut as Ryan continued to stroke him,

Braxton shook his head. "Two days of you torturing me with sex isn't gonna scare me away."

"No?" Ryan liked hearing that, but he had to push a little bit. His sub shouldn't find him too predictable. And some fear could bring a nice edge to their play. "What if I decide to introduce you to a flogger? Or a whip? Or lock you in a cage to rely on me for everything you eat and drink, only letting you out to relieve yourself? There are many things I'd like to try with you and I can be quite creative."

If anything, what had been intended as a warning only intensified the heat in Braxton's eyes. "Sounds hot."

Could he be any more perfect?

"Nothing I do will ever impact your play or training, but we can work around that." Ryan slid his lips over Braxton's dick, taking him in deep without warning, giving him a slap on his inner thigh when he began to thrust up. As the young man stilled, he quickened his pace, bringing Braxton right to the edge, then easing back and casually continuing the conversation as Braxton caught his breath. "There are also many Doms on the team who can advise me on limits for you. When I bring you to the club, I may have them observe for the first few times. I may be able to manage most submissives, but I've never been with an athlete."

"You'd let them watch you…do stuff to me?"

"Would you like that?"

Braxton's row furrowed. "I don't know. I'm not exactly out to everyone."

"Neither am I, so don't worry if you're not ready. That will come at your pace or not at all." Ryan would also have to consider his own approach with revealing his sexuality to his peers. And his family. It had never seemed important before, but he refused to hide Braxton if their relationship developed any further. If Braxton was comfortable with people knowing about them, Ryan would figure out how to do the same. "I'm pleased with how open you are with me."

"You make it easy, Rya—Sir." Braxton inhaled slowly. "I mean, the talking part. The not begging? Not so much."

Wrapping his hand around Braxton's dick, Ryan glanced up at him, brow raised. "And if I let you beg, what would you ask for?"

There was no hesitation in Braxton's words. "You to fuck me. I miss feeling you everywhere. But the way you touch me is so fucking good, I want that too. I want everything."

There was something so pure about the way Braxton responded to him, which was damn refreshing. How Ryan had missed that before, he wasn't sure, but he wanted to hold on to it for as long as possible. He'd been given a gift when the young man had walked back into his life and he wouldn't take that for granted.

He climbed over Braxton, settling between his thighs as he picked up the bottle of lube. Pouring a generous amount in his palm, he slicked up his fingers, using his knees to spread Braxton's thighs. He brought his fingers to the tight hole, teasing the tip of one inside until Braxton was shaking with the struggle to hold still.

Such a well behaved little sub already. He'd be fun to play with, to keep testing until restraints were needed because containing himself became too overwhelming. Next time Ryan had him here, he'd put new cuffs on him.

And his collar would look fucking hot around Braxton's neck.

Leaning in, he filled Braxton with one finger, letting him adjust before adding a second. Once he had him groaning, thighs tensing against the urge to move with the motions of his fingers, Ryan removed them. He grabbed the condom, rolling it over his dick, then hooked his arm under Braxton's knee as he positioned himself and watched the head of his cock stretch him open.

Gripping the pillow behind him, Braxton tipped his head back and let out a low moan as Ryan filled him, inch by inch. He rocked his hips, taking Braxton deeper, never shifting his gaze from where his dick slid in all the way, then disappeared inside the snug heat of the other man's body.

Pleasure gathered within and he gave in, letting it drive his pace as he clenched the muscles of his ass with harder thrusts, looking up to watch Braxton's face as he fucked him. The sound of him pounding into that tight ass, the breathless gasps coming from the man beneath him, joined his own sharp breaths. He sensed his release coming, much too soon, and let himself slip free.

Then slammed back in.

"Jesus, I love that." Braxton clenched around him, crying out with raw pleasure as Ryan took him deep, making the bed shake with the motion. "Every time your dick stretches back into me it's… Oh God, that. Just like that."

Ryan leaned down to kiss Braxton's parted lips, letting the head of his dick work him open again and again, smiling as Braxton spoke soft, incoherent words, tossing his head from side to side, his hips shifting uncontrollably. He came with a shout and Ryan pistoned into him as he finally let his own release overtake him.

Billowing out with an intensity he'd rarely felt before, his orgasm had all his muscles clenching as he came. The pleasure was heat and pressure within, drawn out until he had to slam his hand down on the mattress to avoid collapsing on top of Braxton.

He held himself tight against Braxton's body and let out a harsh whisper in his ear. "Don't you dare move."

The sparkle in Braxton's eyes showed he was trying very hard not to laugh. Which had him tensing within. Around Ryan's oversensitive dick.

To repay him, Ryan bent down and bit his shoulder. Hard.

"Ouch!" Braxton clenched again, then groaned. "Shit, my dick feels like it wants to get hard again."

Carefully withdrawing from Braxton's body, Ryan looked down at him, his lips slitting into a smile that usually made subs very nervous.

And Braxton was no exception.

"W-what?" Braxton's throat worked as he swallowed. "There's no way I could—"

"One of the benefits of being young, pet." Ryan didn't have much strength yet, but he'd find enough to deal with his naughty sub. And he'd enjoy every fucking minute. "I may need time to recover. But you don't."

Reaching into the drawer in his night stand where he kept all his favorite toys, each one meticulously clean and ready for moments like this, Ryan pulled out a long, thick black butt plug.

Braxton's eyes went wide.

"You can use your safeword, Braxton. Or you can be my good boy and thank your Dom for seeing to your pleasure." Ryan tapped the tip of the buttplug against Braxton's thigh. "Will you come for me again?"

For a moment, Ryan was sure Braxton would refuse. Or at least continue insisting that he couldn't.

Instead, he wet his bottom lip with his tongue and nodded. "Yes, Sir. Thank you."

Curving his hand under Braxton's jaw, Ryan gave him a long, slow kiss.

"That's my good boy."

CHAPTER 13

Humming to himself, Braxton put on another load of laundry, separating everything like his mother had taught him, then reading the instructions on the fabric softener to make sure he was using it right. Ryan had taken a nap after making Braxton come several times with his mouth and hands and a butt plug he insisted was one of the smallest ones he had.

Braxton wasn't sure he wanted to see the others.

As much as he'd enjoyed every fucking minute of Ryan working him over, and as worn out as his body was from so many forced orgasms, nothing was as satisfying as having Ryan against him, thrusting deep into his body. Or even taking the man's dick in his mouth and watching pleasure darken his features as he used Braxton to get him off.

Ryan's approval and satisfaction had quickly become more important than Braxton's own and he loved when Ryan gave him commands that helped him fulfill those urges. Being introduced to his submissive side felt like the most natural thing in the world. And exploring it with Ryan everything he could've ever wanted. There was a closeness between them he'd never found with anyone, a connection that strengthened the one they'd had after knowing one another for only a few hours.

He'd already known he wouldn't be able to forget Ryan. Now? He couldn't picture his life without him.

Pulling the dry clothes out of the dryer and putting them in the wicker basket he'd found with some folded clothes already inside, he turned to bring it to the living room where he could fold it while watching the sports highlights.

His heart skipped a few beats at the sight of Ryan, leaning against the doorway, thumbs hooked to the pocket of his jeans and a smile on his lips.

"I'd take exception to you being dressed, but I'm more interested in what it is you're doing." Ryan nodded at the basket. "Have you decided to explore the service side of submission or was the pile of laundry getting too big?"

Braxton snickered at the last and shook his head. "There was barely enough for two small loads." He shrugged and lowered his gaze. "I enjoy doing things that make you happy."

Ryan's expression warmed as he pushed away from the doorframe and came toward Braxton, tipping up his chin with a finger and claiming his lips in a deep kiss that stole all the air from the room. A warmth filled Braxton's chest and he couldn't help see how domestic this all was. Which he'd been afraid Ryan wouldn't want, but he'd have said so, wouldn't he?

"Come on, we'll fold them together and I'll order some pizza for lunch." Ryan pulled his phone out of his pocket and used an app to place the order. "I have one day left with you, and as much as I'd enjoy one less chore, I'll get restless if I have to sit there and watch."

Braxton's lips curved. "And you also need to make sure I do it exactly how you like it."

With a wry grin, Ryan inclined his head. "Yes, there's that too."

In the living room, Braxton set the basket on the floor by the coffee table and sat next to it. While Ryan searched for something on TV to watch, he began folding towels. The first one didn't look horrible, but the next was a completely different shape. He frowned and started over.

Better this time, but still…

"I am not that anal, Braxton."

Biting into his bottom lip to hold back a laugh, Braxton glanced over at the other man.

Who shook his head and chuckled. "Brat. You know what I mean. Here, pass me one."

Spreading the towel on the coffee table, Ryan folded it along the length, then along the width, then in three. When Braxton did the next one—much slower because he wanted it to turn out just as nice and neat—he was happy to see the simple method worked for him too. He fixed the first towel he'd done, then piled them all together.

"Very nice." Ryan curved his hand around the back of Braxton's neck, stroking the length of his throat lightly with his thumb. "I could get used to this."

A cozy sensation of pure joy flowed over Braxton, surrounding him like a blanket straight out of the dryer being wrapped around him on a cold winter night. He'd been worried about bringing up anything that sounded too long term, even though Ryan seemed open to the idea of dating. There was starting a relationship, and there was *"I never want to leave your side."*

As much as his intense feelings for Ryan had him leaning toward the latter, he knew better than to voice those words. If this was going to last, he couldn't rush things. He'd hit his quota of acting crazy already.

Ryan tightened his grip on the back of Braxton's neck. "You

will tell me what suddenly has you looking so serious." He glanced toward the door at a knock. "After I get the pizza."

The warm, mouthwatering scent of fresh bread, melted cheese, bacon, and spicy sauce filled the room as Ryan carried the pizza in, waiting for Braxton to set all the towels in the basket before placing the box, along with two cans of root beer, on the table.

Opening the box, Ryan considered Braxton for a moment. "I'd feed you, but I've found that rather difficult to do with pizza. Hot pizza sauce on your naked chest wouldn't be as sexy as it sounds."

"That does not sound sexy at all."

Pulling a piece of pizza free, Ryan shot him a crooked grin. "I'd lick it off and make you feel all better."

"I don't think I should be eating naked. Ever. This is starting to sound dangerous." He gave a fake shudder at the idea of hot pizza sauce anywhere else, but his dick was not thinking of the potential pain. Groaning, he shifted as it hardened. "Do not consider this interest."

Bursting out laughing as Braxton pointed at his dick, Ryan nodded toward the pizza. "Eat. You'll need your energy. I promise not to eat anything off of you that will give you second degree burns."

"That should be much more reassuring than it is."

"Mhmm." Ryan took a bite of pizza, watching Braxton do the same. He put his piece of pizza on the lid of the pizza box and opened his can of root beer, taking a few gulps before he spoke again. "I will never do lasting damage to you, pet. If it's too hot to go on my own body, it's not going on yours."

Fuck, now he was thinking of licking things off Ryan. He ducked his head, taking a big bite of pizza, wincing as the sauce burnt his tongue.

"Slow down. I won't put up with you hurting yourself either."

Braxton swallowed and took a sip of soda. "Then you probably don't want to watch my games."

"I won't be missing a single one." Ryan smiled and reached out, wiping a bit of sauce off of Braxton's chin with his thumb. "I avoided any mention of hockey after I met you. You were hard enough not to think of without dealing with constant reminders. Now…I think I'll enjoy them."

If his heart swelled any bigger, he was going to pass out once he hit the ice. He polished off two slices of pizza before Ryan's expectant look had him wondering if he'd dazed off and missed something.

Ryan picked up a napkin and cleaned the grease off his fingers. "You had a very serious expression before. Was something bothering you?"

Damn, Braxton had hoped he'd forgotten about that. He shook his head and grabbed his soda. "I was just thinking about how things will be once I get back. Being here this long is awesome, but obviously we can't do that all the time. I mean, I got my own place."

"Yes, you do. And I work long shifts and wouldn't feel comfortable with you being here alone." Ryan held up his hand when Braxton's lips parted. "Not because of you. I wouldn't have continued sleeping when you got out of bed if I didn't trust you in my home. My life can be dangerous at times. I won't put you at risk."

"I can take care of myself, Ryan."

"Under normal circumstances? Sure. Against bikers with guns?" Ryan gave him a level look. "Be reasonable. I want to see you as often as we're both able. And I have no problem going to your apartment now and then." His lips quirked. "But after what you told me, you're buying new towels."

"Deal." Braxton grinned, grabbing another piece of pizza and leaning against Ryan's legs as he put The Office on. His eyes drifted shut as Ryan began stroking his hair and everything was just…so fucking good. He couldn't really explain it.

The sex was amazing, but moments like this were what made him believe their crazy schedules and lifestyles and living situations wouldn't get in the way of what they were building. Ryan was becoming his Dom, but they could still discuss things. He'd never been so happy just being around someone.

He was a bit sleepy again and his eyes kept drifting shut, but he tried to force himself to stay awake. He didn't want to miss out on any time with Ryan, even if they were only lazing around, watching TV.

Movement behind him had him sitting up as Ryan stretched out on the sofa, then patted the cushion. It was a tight squeeze, but Braxton managed to lay down on his side, his back against Ryan's chest. The blanket Ryan pulled over them both wasn't going to help him stay awake, but he realized it didn't matter.

Ryan had been thinking about how things would be between them too. He'd be watching Braxton play. They'd find a way to keep in touch while Braxton was on the road. Maybe meet for lunch when Ryan had long shifts.

When he left tomorrow it wouldn't be the end of what they had together.

They were still at the beginning.

Brushing his lips along Braxton's throat, Ryan spoke softly. "No more stripping on stage. And no more fucking your friends. Understood?"

Eyes closed, Braxton nodded. "I'm good with that. Made me feel like shit anyway."

"That's a shame." Ryan kissed behind his ear and let out a soft laugh. "But I still want details."

CHAPTER 14

The last day off. And his last day with Braxton for the near future. Ryan sat at the kitchen table, enjoying a cup of coffee his boy had made for him perfectly, and observed the other man moving around his kitchen in nothing but an apron. Fuck, but he could get used to this. Using a YouTube video, Braxton was making French toast with a side of bacon and hashbrowns and it smelled amazing. His tight ass on display under the thick, dark blue apron tie made Ryan hungry for something other than food, but if he indulged now, the food would burn.

And Braxton was trying so hard to please him. Hell, since yesterday, aside from laundry, he'd cleaned and dusted almost everything. The peaceful expression on his face, the way he smiled at Ryan's praise, meant so much more than the convenience of having a few less chores to do.

He'd tried, several times, to make plans to enjoy Braxton's presence here more often, but news of one of his bigger cases being botched by the prosecutor and the perp walking free was like a bucket of ice water over them all. The reality was, it just wasn't fucking safe.

But he'd go to Braxton. Make sure there was no way to connect them until the worst threats were gone. Then...hell, if they were still together by then, he'd consider a more permanent arrangement.

"Your breakfast is served, sir." Braxton laid the plate in front of him with a bit of flourish, his graceful movements making it obvious why he'd drawn so much attention on that stage. After filling Ryan's cup with coffee in a French Press Ryan hadn't even known he owned, the man wiggled his hips and went to his own seat, the perfect image of a sub tempting their Dom in a way that would either earn them a spanking or a hard fuck.

Ryan arched a brow at him. "If I have to put you in your place and my food gets cold, I might not be able to keep my promise about what I do to you not impacting your play."

Braxton cocked his head, mischief in his eyes. "Might be worth it."

"I'd make certain it wasn't." Ryan cut into his French toast and took a bite, moaning at the perfect balance of flavor on his tongue. He'd had some doubts about YouTube being useful for cooking, but not anymore. "This is delicious."

Digging into his own food, Braxton nodded. "I like cooking, but I was always worried I wouldn't be any good at it. Using videos helped me make some really good stuff, so I have a few cooking channels I follow to learn from."

"Clever." Ryan added some cream and sugar to his coffee, studying Braxton over the rim. "Do you cook for yourself a lot?"

That gave Braxton pause. He wrinkled his nose and shook his head. "Not really. Now and then if I want to try something, but it's not the same eating by yourself. When I hang out with other players, someone's usually ordering pizza."

"You don't have friends who aren't on the team?"

"I…" Braxton took a deep breath and sat back. "No, I guess I don't. I mean, I had some on my junior team. And back home, but we drifted apart. Hopefully I can stay on this team long enough to really get to know people in the area. Over the summer or something."

"There's a very active local kink community that could be good for that as well." Ryan hadn't become involved much himself, not wanting to risk the guys at the station knowing more about his life than he cared to share, but he wouldn't mind showing Braxton off a bit. The idea had him caring less about what anyone else would think. "Maybe when we both have time, we can go to some of the events."

Wide eyes met his. "Really? I'd love that!"

"Good, I'll look into it while you're on your road trip." He gave Braxton's shoulder a nudge when his smile faded. "This will be our first test of how we'll manage with weeks apart. I'm not worried, so you shouldn't be."

With a slow nod, Braxton squared his shoulders. "Okay. And phone sex could be hot as fuck."

Ryan chuckled. "I wouldn't know."

The mischief was back in Braxton's eyes, he took another bite of French toast, leaning forward once his mouth was clear and licking a droplet of syrup from his bottom lip. "Think about it. I get back to the hotel after a game and lock myself in the bathroom since rookies have to share with a vet. Gotta be quiet so no one knows what I'm doing. I turn the camera on so you can see me...and make me do whatever you want."

All right, that did sound hot. Ryan's lips slanted. "I could torture you and bring you to the edge for days. Refuse to let you come until you return to me."

Face flushed, pupils dilated, Braxton swallowed hard. "Yeah, you totally could."

"Finish your food, boy." Ryan smiled as Braxton stared at him like he'd spoken a foriegn language. "It won't be quite as fun if you anticipate all the terrible ways I could twist remote access in my favor."

Wetting his lips with his tongue, Braxton looked both fascinated and a little afraid. Perfect. He'd probably be very worked up by the time he was able to make the call. Eager for anything Ryan planned, his mind going over all best and worst case scenarios. It would definitely help keep the power exchange going while they were apart.

By the time he'd finished the amazing meal, Ryan's thoughts had drifted to another matter they hadn't discussed at length. Braxton mentioning locking himself in the bathroom sounded like something he did regularly. Of all the lessons he'd taught Braxton over the past few days, this one would be the most difficult to implement.

But also the most satisfying.

Leaving Braxton to tidy up the kitchen—despite his own typical need to clean when someone else cooked, as his mother had instilled on him—Ryan went to his room to get what he'd need. When he returned Braxton was hand washing the dishes. Unnecessary, since there was a dishwasher for the task, but he seemed like he was in the zone. Their time was running out and he was soaking in every last bit of submission he could. Offering his Dom all he could think of with his limited knowledge of the lifestyle.

It was beautiful to watch. That sweet, serene look on his face. The way his eyes shone when he looked over at Ryan.

And the little smile on his lips as Ryan came up behind him and kissed the back of his neck. He continued washing the dishes, a plate slipping in his hand before he tightened his grip. His breaths came out in little pants when he heard the top pop on the lube. He began to press back, anticipating Ryan's next move…

Then caught on when Ryan moved away. Held still. And waited.

He was everything. This journey with him would be incredible, no matter where either of them were. They'd find a way to keep this connection between them growing stronger.

But he'd use every last moment that remained to solidify the foundation they'd built.

He let out a soft laugh and whispered in Braxton's ear. "Do you know what it means to be mine?"

CHAPTER 15

Part of Braxton was already missing this time with Ryan, but his Dom brought him back to the present with his touch. With his way of grounding him with his tone, until all he had to let go and follow his command. That would be true no matter where he was.

But he was here. Now.

"I didn't tell you to stop."

Sucking in a breath at the warning in Ryan's tone, Braxton retrieved the plate he'd dropped. Almost let it slip from his grip again as Ryan reached around him, securing a cock ring under his balls and at the base of his cock. God, the way the man took ownership of his body pushed all the right buttons. How he assumed control as though it was the natural order of things. The headspace Braxton found with him, the pure bliss of surrender was unmatched by anything short of a winning goal at the final moments of a tied game, and even then…

The faint apple scent of the soap reached him with every quick inhale as he braced himself, while scrubbing the plate more than it needed. He rinsed it off, lips parting as Ryan pressed into him, his dick stretching him open, bit at a time, not shifting him enough to disrupt his task. One hand on the edge of the sink, he tipped his hips back, needing that fullness to take him completely.

"No." Ryan chuckled, using the spatula Braxton had just washed to smack his thigh hard enough to leave a little sting. "This isn't for you to take, my boy. This is me giving you as much or as little as I choose to. We'll see if it's enough for you."

A test. One Braxton would pass, no matter how hard it was. He thought back on their conversation and had to bite back a groan. Would Ryan really edge him until he came back from the road trip?

Holy fuck, that's...kinda hot. If torture can be considered hot. There was no way he wouldn't feel Ryan with him every moment of every day if all the relief he'd get would be withheld until he returned to him. He groaned as Ryan took him deeper, dragging in and out at a languorous pace, stimulating parts of him the man already knew better than Braxton knew himself. He'd be able to bring back this sensation with a thought.

With a word.

During a call when Ryan would give him only enough to remind him of what was waiting for him.

"I can see you understand." Ryan gripped Braxton's hips, driving in hard, kissing his shoulder when he let out a rough, desperate sound. "Being mine won't always be easy, but it doesn't need to be. Not for you. You enjoy a challenge and I'm going to give you one."

Another dish, this one a cup, the handle the only thing that kept Braxton from dropping it as he struggled to wash it while Ryan fucked him in long, hard strokes. The way the man used him was a rush, just knowing he'd find pleasure in Braxton's body, that he knew he could take that and it would be enough.

The satisfaction didn't come from reaching some kind of end. There was no end. That was the point.

Once the last of the dishes were washed, Ryan finally let him hold on to the counter, slamming into him over and over, the sound of the hard smacks he landed on Braxton's thighs, the slap of his pelvis against Braxton's ass, filling the kitchen along with the faint sounds of the morning outside. Cars passing. Birds, the rustle of the wind. The pressure within coiled, tighter and tighter, and pleasure played through him like a melody bringing it all together on a loop.

"There we go." Ryan pistoned in and out, his voice rough as he came closer to finding his own release. His grip on Braxton's hips was bruising, giving him another mark he could use as a reminder when the space between them seemed too much. He was giving Braxton everything he'd need to believe they could make this work. "Being mine means you'll always have this, my boy. The feeling of me with you. It won't always be easy. But it'll be worth it."

Panting, Braxton let himself go, not needing to come to take everything Ryan gave him and lose himself to it. He hovered a bit above himself, his body jerking as his body tried to take more, grateful that Ryan had cut off the option. The ache within was a bit painful, but nothing compared to the satisfaction when Ryan pressed close to him, kissing his shoulder and his neck, heat spilling deep within.

Ryan stroked Braxton's thigh, easing away before removing the condom and disposing of it in the trash. "You're going to keep that cockring. Put it on whenever we're on a call that's long enough to get...interesting."

His whole body jerking as Ryan unclipped the length of leather, Braxton nodded. "Yes, sir. I can do that." His cheeks heated as he tried to picture being quiet while having phone sex with Ryan, edging for over a week. "Focusing on the game while I'm dying to get back to you is going to be tricky."

Washing his hands, Ryan glanced over and arched a brow at him. "You do know I'll be watching you, yes? Consider wanting to impress me more than how horny you'll be."

"I will, sir." Braxton closed his eyes as his Dom rewarded him with a deep kiss. Relaxed in the strong arms that wrapped around him. "Besides, you being distracted could be dangerous. Now that I think about it… Yeah, no losing focus. We can have this and...and everything else."

Drawing back, Ryan cupped his cheek. "We can. But I'll miss you. I'll be looking forward to our calls. Don't think I don't understand that I'm asking a lot of you. If I didn't think you could do it, I wouldn't even consider taking this thing between us any further."

Braxton smiled, still feeling Ryan's touch even as he moved away. Whatever else they faced, so they were on the same page concerning their relationship. And it was a damn good place to be. "I'm happy you are." He made a face as he checked the time on the microwave. "I should start getting ready."

"Yes. And you'll have to take a cab back to your place. I'd rather drive you myself, but…" Ryan sighed and shook his head. "I won't take any chances with you."

The first time they'd had this discussion, Braxton couldn't help arguing, but this time, he accepted Ryan's decision and the reasons behind it without question. He shifted forward, stealing a kiss and snickered when Ryan smacked his ass. "If you can put up with the craziness of my job, I can deal with whatever comes with yours."

"That's good to hear, my boy." Ryan brushed a hand over his hair, a tenderness in his eyes. "I can't tell you exactly when I'll call, but I have a general idea of when you'll be available. If you try to call me and I don't answer, I'm probably on duty."

"I'm allowed to call you too?"

Ryan gave him a level look. "Within reason. And don't call my sister if you don't hear from me."

"No, sir. I've learned my lesson." Braxton went to the bedroom, feeling Ryan's eyes on him as he got dressed. "If...if anything happens, someone will let me know though, right?"

For a long time it seemed like Ryan had no intention of answering. But then he put his hand on Braxton's shoulder. Met his eyes when he turned. "Yes, Braxton. I won't leave you wondering. I'm going to be telling Laura about you soon, and if not her, someone else will be in touch if there's ever an emergency. I'd like you to make the same arrangements. Accidents happen on the ice and I don't want to be left waiting to hear whatever the team decides to tell the press."

That was more than fair. Braxton inhaled slowly, hoping neither of them would even need to get that call, but finding some comfort in the fact that what they had was special enough to make these kinds of plans. "I will, sir."

The rest of the day seemed almost surreal with how normal it was, but it wasn't until he'd said goodbye and was in the cab that it really hit him. Usually, road trips were exciting and he didn't think too much about how long they'd last. Everything that really mattered in his life was around him, everything he'd worked so hard for, all his hopes and dreams were along for the ride. He'd never let himself want more.

He still had all he'd accomplished. Still had his goals and Ryan wouldn't let him lose sight of them.

But now, on top of the excitement of the game…

Was something else. Something beyond the thrill of every win.

There was a reason to look forward to coming home.

CHAPTER 16

Ryan never denied being a workaholic. He loved investigating cases, often brought them home with him, and he put in as many extra hours as humanly possible. But...being with Braxton changed that. He found himself watching the clock, eager to get home even when his boy was on the road, because either he could watch him play, or see him on video. On his days off he checked flights, knowing a spontaneous trip wouldn't be practical, but hell was he tempted.

Somehow, in the weeks apart, he and Braxton had grown closer. Not because of the phone sex—though that definitely spiced things up—but he'd never shared so much of his life, his thoughts and dreams and random observations, with anyone. Or been so interested in every single detail of someone else's life. Hearing his phone buzz, seeing Braxton's number, never failed to make him smile.

There was no mistaking it. He was falling hard and fast, but he didn't bother putting his hands out to brace himself. He couldn't stop it. And didn't want to.

Not when he looked into Braxton's eyes and knew he felt the same.

With so many away games, there wasn't much time to spend together. When Braxton had returned this past weekend, their schedules clashed to the point that the only way they'd been able to see one another was for Ryan to swing by the forum between practice and that night's game to take his boy out to lunch.

This week wasn't looking to be much different, but Ryan would deal. So long as he got to hold Braxton, hear his laugh up close, taste the sweetness of his lips…

Yeah, he was getting sappy as fuck over a man who should have been all wrong for him.

And he couldn't care less.

Tonight, stepping into his empty house had him thinking about the long summer ahead and an idea he'd been toying with. One so reckless he'd shelved it because he knew he needed to go back to his old ways, at least in part, and weigh the pros and cons.

He wanted Braxton here. In his bed whenever he could be. His clothes in Ryan's closet, his favorite food in his cupboard, his stinky gym bag tossed in the garage until it could be decontaminated.

The problem was, it was too soon. Ryan's life wasn't safe. He was stuck in his ways and...all right, the last wasn't true. He'd believed it once, but having Braxton around proved he could be adaptable. Willing to compromise. Be spontaneous and find joy in all the little things that had passed him by before.

Sighing, he tossed his bag of takeout on the coffee table, turning on the TV before he sat, the station already set to the game. He relaxed onto the sofa, smiling a bit at the sound of skates on ice. Recognized several of the players from interactions over the years. Some closer than others, like Tyler Vanek and Raif Zovko, both in a polyam relationship with Laura and

Chicklet. There'd been some ups and downs, but his sister seemed happy now, so he didn't question the complexity. Tyler was a handful, but Raif and Chicklet managed him well enough. And the young man brought some fun into Ryan's sister's life.

She deserved that. She deserved what all of them gave her.

Gaze scanning the screen, Ryan went through his usual routine of searching for Braxton. His boy wasn't on the ice yet. Frowning, he sat forward, checking out the players still on the bench. Usually, Braxton was one of the first out there. He didn't get long shifts like the higher ranking players, but he was starting to be used more often on the penalty kill, which he'd been excited about. And being on the bench for most of the game meant he took every opportunity to stretch his legs.

The screen switched to the announcers without Ryan spotting Braxton. He took a big bite of his burger, hardly tasting it as he listened to them go on about expectations for the night. Players being called up last minute because of injuries, but Braxton wasn't mentioned.

Then one of the male sports reporters held up his hand. "Just coming in, we have another player out of the lineup. This appears to have been a game time decision by the team doctor. We'll share more details as soon as we have them."

As the chatter continued on to other things, Ryan couldn't hear a single word. He set down his burger and pulled out his phone, checking to see if he'd missed Braxton's call. Nothing. Shaking his head, he opened the can of rootbeer that had come with his meal, already dialing. When Braxton didn't answer, he called Laura.

Her tone was cheerful as she answered. "Hey! I hope you're calling just for the hell of it, and not because you want me to cancel your visit to see Mom and Dad this weekend for you, because it's not happening. They've been planning this for months."

"No, it's not that…" Ryan had been looking forward to seeing their parents. He'd planned to tell them about Braxton. And...well, the fact that he was gay. He didn't see it being a huge issue, more them being concerned that he hadn't told them sooner. With the hell Laura had been through with her birth mother, it had seemed ridiculous to act like his sexuality was even something that needed to be addressed.

Avoiding the subject at work had also led to avoiding it in general, but that was a bit harder to explain. Still, of all people, Laura would probably be hurt that he hadn't confided in her.

He took a deep breath. "I wanted to know if you'd heard anything about what's going on with Braxton. He's...out of the lineup."

There was a long silence. "Braxton...Richards? As in the hockey player?"

"Laura—"

"No, give me a second, I'm trying to understand why in the world this would be on your radar." Laura's voice tightened a bit. "Since when do you care about the games, or the players, or… Ryan…"

Damn it, this wasn't how he should be telling her, but he'd waited too long. And he needed to know what was happening with Braxton, not spend half the call beating around the fucking bush. "I'm gay, Laura. I've been seeing him...hell, it's been a couple of months now, but it started...a while ago. I wasn't sure how to tell you—I knew I could, it's just…"

Laura exhaled roughly. "Wow, my big brother, not sounding sure of himself for once. You've got it bad. I can't even be upset." She let out a soft laugh. "I should've suspected something when he was getting my number from Tyler to talk to you."

"He's too young, I know." Ryan rubbed his hand over his mouth, expecting the lecture, logic not really kicking in. Tyler wasn't that much older.

This time, Laura chuckled. "He's an adult and he clearly knows exactly what—and *who*—he wants. But I won't torture you. Give me a few minutes, I'll see if I can get a hold of Oriana. She went on the road with them and she'll know what's up."

"Thank you." Letting out a sigh of relief, Ryan tipped his head back. "Hell, this was easier than I thought it would be. I was expecting to feel guilty. I should've known better."

That got him a sharp laugh. "Oh, I'm not done with you yet, big brother. Save it. We'll get there when you're not worried about your man. I love you. Bye."

After the line clicked off, Ryan smiled a little, knowing Laura was only teasing. His sister could hold a grudge like no one's business, but he could tell when she was really upset. She didn't hold back. In this case, she'd likely want to talk things over, but more than anyone, she'd understand him hesitating, for any reason.

Which didn't stop him from checking his phone every five minutes, waiting for her to call him back. He managed to eat a bit more, but the food was tasteless. For some reason, his mind kept going to worst case scenarios. There was no way Braxton wouldn't call him if he could. The young man was many things, but thoughtless wasn't one of them. He knew how closely Ryan watched his games. That he'd be concerned when he didn't see Braxton out there.

About half an hour passed before his phone rang.

"I need you to listen to everything I have to say before you freak out." Laura's soothing tone only put Ryan more on edge, but he didn't interrupt because he needed whatever information she had *now*. "Braxton was feeling off this morning, but like all players, he pushed through it. No one knew anything was up until just before the game. Sloan caught him swaying on his skates and pulled him aside. He was running a fever. It was really high, so they sent him to the hospital. The flu's been going around, so they think it's that."

Ryan braced his head on his hand, elbow on the kitchen table where he'd finally stopped pacing. "Are they sending him home?"

A pause, then Laura sighed. "Not yet. He was dehydrated and they want to keep him a few days because of some complications. The team makes sure the players always have the best doctors, Ryan. He's in good hands."

But he's not with me.

Nodding slowly, Ryan sat back in his chair. "I guess he'll have friends or family there with him?"

That got him a longer silence. "Both his parents are in the military and aren't due back for months. Braxton has a request that no one contact them unless it's life or death. Sloan and a few other players will check in on him when they can, before the team continues on the road. He'll be sent home as soon as the doctors feel he's up to it."

In other words...Braxton will be alone.

Like hell.

Ryan pushed to his feet, then headed to his bedroom. He grabbed an overnight bag from his closet. "Text me the name of the hospital and his room number. Tell Callahan I'm on my way so I'll be cleared to see him."

"Are you serious? Ryan, think about what you're doing." Laura sounded stunned. "If you're not careful, you'll out him...*and* yourself. Are you ready for that? Are you sure he is?"

Bag open on his bed, Ryan began tossing in what he'd need for the next few days. "If he's not, I'll do what I have to so this is kept private. I'm sure the team will cooperate, not all the queer players on the team are out. We'll take this at his pace."

With a quiet sigh, Laura seemed ready to try a different approach, but she was too straightforward to pussyfoot around the issues. "I can tell you care about him very much, but this all seems...very fast for you. I'm not going to lie, I can't wrap my head around you taking leave at a moment's notice and hopping on a plane to look after a man you've been dating mostly long distance for two months."

A smile tugged at Ryan's lips, despite the concern constricting his chest and his need to keep moving so he could get to Braxton as soon as possible. "Because it's not something I was ever willing to do for anyone except you and our parents. I wasn't willing to take chances or let anyone in, I thought I had everything I could ever want. But I was wrong. And one man showed me that, in little ways at first. Ways I didn't see coming until it was too late to put my guard up. And by the time I realized it'd happened? I didn't want to. I wanted him. And this relationship deserves better than to do anything halfway. *He* deserves better from me."

"All right, despite my reservations, I really love hearing that. I never said anything about you being alone, because you seemed to prefer it that way, but you're a good man, Ryan." Laura exhauled on a laugh. "Mom and Dad are going to be excited to meet him. I hope you'll let me be there when you share the good news. And I'll let Sloan know you're on your way."

"Thank you." Ryan zipped up his suitcase. "I love you, sis. Wish me luck on getting a damn flight out to New York tonight because I won't be able to sit still until I know he's okay."

There was the sound of a soft breeze over the line, as though Laura had stepped outside. "I love you too. And I'd tell you again that he'll be fine, but I get it. It's not the same hearing it as seeing it for yourself."

After exchanging goodbye's and promises to call with updates, Ryan hung up, then began his search for the next flight out. One connection in Montreal, then straight to LaGuardia. Leaving in less than two hours.

Cursing under his breath, Ryan secured the ticket, then

hurried out to his car. A cab would be a better idea, and cheaper in the long run, but he needed this bit of control over when he left and how fast he got to the airport. Such a small thing to keep himself from obsessing over what might go wrong.

Braxton was young. Healthy. An athlete in the best condition he'd ever be in.

And yet, something felt...off.

There was no way Braxton would've pretended to be fine just to play, was there? Yes, probably, that seemed to be a common thing with hockey players. Which didn't make it right. Ryan might not have any say about Braxton's career, but they would discuss the risks Braxton would take for it, if he *had* ignored his own health just to get in some extra playing time.

The thing was, the more Ryan thought about it, the more he doubted that had been the case. Knowing Braxton, this had to be something different. Something unexpected.

Whatever it was—*God, don't let it be anything serious*—Ryan would be there with him as he faced it. And for every step going forward.

Laura was right about one thing. He'd never done impulsive. Never dived into a situation where he couldn't be sure of all possible outcomes. Never let his heart lead the way. This had never been the type of man Ryan was.

But it was the type of man he wanted to be.

For the man he loved.

CHAPTER 17

If this had been the flu, Braxton would've never complained about having to get vaccines again. Hell, he probably wouldn't anyway. He was rarely sick. He'd rather keep it that way.

Unfortunately, going from being real healthy all the time to *this?*

He'd never seen a doctor for more than a checkup. Never had to be admitted to the hospital for anything. With good insurance to cover him while he traveled and a team behind him, he was luckier than most, but...

Right now, he didn't feel that way at all.

He was alone.

And terrified.

The doctor had asked him a bunch of questions when he'd gotten here, but everything was confusing and Braxton wasn't sure any of his answers made sense. His head hurt worse than the last time he'd gotten a concussion and his stomach felt like it'd been turned inside-out from how sick he'd been—he hadn't drank any alcohol in weeks, so it definitely wasn't a hangover.

His neck being stiff seemed to shift things into high gear. Before they'd even started the test, he was put on an IV. The doctor explained what he was doing, but Braxton couldn't follow.

Then there were needles. One in his spine which was pure fucking torture.

Everyone was wearing masks.

Hours later, he was dozing in a private room when the door opened. Eyes burning, he tried to sit up, vision blurry, shaking his head as a nurse spoke softly to him. At first he couldn't make out a thing she said.

But he heard a name.

A sob broke from his throat. "Ryan? You have to call him. Tell him not to worry. I would've told him, but I didn't get a—"

"Shh…" A soft touch, on the back of his hand. That familiar presence. Eyes he'd stared into from his knees, above him, hazy, but close enough he could see the smile in them above the blue medical mask. "I know you would've, my sweet man. It's okay, I know this wasn't something you could help. Try to rest."

Checking his chart, the nurse, who's name tag read simply 'Amanda', had a brightness to her tone. "Your partner insisted on seeing you, Braxton. The doctor is allowing it, but he'll need to keep that mask on whenever he's here for the next twenty-four hours. He won't be able to stay overnight tonight, but tomorrow night will be fine."

The way Ryan tensed made it obvious that he wasn't thrilled with the idea of leaving at all, but his tone was pleasant when he regarded the nurse. "I appreciate that. I still think I'd be fine just staying up to watch over him."

"Mhm." Amanda lowered her dark brows at him, the elastic from the mask leaving red marks on her light brown skin. "But he needs his rest. And so, I suspect, do you, Detective. If you want to be well enough to take care of him, it's best to reduce any risks."

"Risks?" Braxton tried to pull his hand away from Ryan's, but didn't have the strength to get far. "What's wrong with me? Am I going to make him sick? Or my team?"

Shaking her head, Amanda jotted a few things on the chart with a pen from her pocket. "No, but several of your teammates who might have shared your water bottles during recent practices will be given a prophylaxis treatment as a precaution."

It was rare bottle mix ups happened for this exact reason, but not impossible. Braxton winced as he thought of how quick the rookies could be sometimes to grab whatever bottle was closest. "So this is contagious, but only...only certain ways?"

"Yes. Bacterial meningitis tends to spread quickly through dorms and other shared living spaces. It's very serious, but the doctor said this was caught early, which gives you a better chance at a full recovery." Amanda checked the line on his IV. "Right now, the most important thing is for you to sleep and let the antibiotics do their work."

Braxton nodded, relaxing back against the pillows. "How soon will I be able to get back on the ice?"

Amusement shone in Amanda's eyes as she exchanged a look with Ryan, holding up her hand when he huffed. "Let's get you through the hard part first. Doctor Davids will consult with the team doctors on your recovery plan, depending on how things go over the next few days. I can say you should be able to go home by the end of the week."

"Thank you, Amanda." Braxton's cheeks heated even as the nurse inclined her head, then left the room. For some reason, it felt like he should be calling her something else. Something more official. But his last nurse had insisted on just using her first name. He licked his dry lips, then turned his attention to Ryan. "Sir...I'm…" His eyes teared again. "I'm sorry, I know I'm being all pathetic, but I'm so glad you're here. I was so fucking scared."

Clasping his hand, Ryan reached out with the other to wipe away the tears that spilled down Braxton's cheeks with his fingertips. "Nothing could've kept me away when I found out something was wrong. I hoped I wasn't overstepping by asking my sister to get in touch with your coach, but at the same time..." He chuckled. "It wouldn't be the first time one of us used those tactics. Fair play and all."

The reminder of when Braxton had gotten in touch with Laura so he could talk to Ryan was embarrassing as hell, but it didn't bother him all that much if these were the results. Just having Ryan close was worth anything he'd have to face next. It was like...like the touch, the voice of the man he'd given his heart to—almost too fast—gave him all the strength he'd ever need.

His brow furrowed as another thought occurred to him. "You weren't out at work. How did you explain coming all the way here, taking time off—"

"I didn't have to, I had plenty of personal time off to collect on. And Sloan told me my being here will be kept private as well." Ryan's gaze turned serious. "I intend to be open with everyone at the station, and with my family, but that's my choice. You're under no obligation to say anything to anyone unless, or until you're ready."

Eyes already drifting shut, his whole body weighed down, Braxton shook his head. "I want them to know. The guys will come before they leave for the next game. You'll be here. I won't lie to them..." He inhaled slowly. "But the nurse said you have to go..."

Tone low, soothing, Ryan held his hand, stroking his palm with his thumb. "Not until you're asleep, and I might even be back before you wake up again. We'll talk about this more tomorrow. For now, do you want to hear about the meal my mother's planning for the next family barbeque? It's always a huge feast. Once she knows about you, she's going to insist I bring you. I can't wait for you to meet both my parents. And my father makes the absolute best ribs on the grill. Almost as good as my mom's. Expect them to ask you what you think, it's their own little competition and she's still the reigning champion..."

As Braxton drifted off, he could practically smell the food as Ryan described it in detail. Hear the laughter of his family members. See the sun set over the ocean while the salty air brushed against his skin. All the fear that had been clinging to him lost its hold, leaving only Ryan's, even when Braxton sensed he was gone.

Like he'd predicted, Ryan was there again when Braxton opened his eyes. Wearing a mask again, but that was okay if it kept him safe. The doctor came and went, explaining the test results and Braxton's ongoing treatment, most of which was hard to follow, but Ryan seemed locked on the man's every word. He asked questions Braxton hadn't even thought of, about long term recovery and things to watch out for.

While Braxton was napping, Ryan must've slipped out, because the next time he opened his eyes his phone and iPad were on the tray next to him. And Ryan had a thick, navy blue robe he wrapped around Braxton's shoulders when he got up to use the bathroom and stretch his legs.

Standing for any length of time made him feel like he'd been doing nonstop shifts on the ice, but Ryan was right there, supporting him, only giving him a hard look once when Braxton said he didn't have to.

"You agreed to submit to me, did you not?" That deep, low voice, one that reached somewhere inside Braxton beyond the last of his weak resistance, accompanied Ryan picking him right up to lay him back on the bed and tuck him in. "That includes more than sex and spankings, my boy. I'm not a doctor, I can't make you all better. This is what I can do for you, and you will let me do it."

Braxton grinned, resting on the pillows as Ryan tucked him back in. "Yes, sir. But I bet, if you could, you'd tell this thing to get the fuck out of me and order me to get better."

"The language on you." Ryan's eyes were smiling again, the mask blowing out with his laugh. "If I had that power, you're damn right I would. I will, however, tend to your every need because it's my right. Now scooch over, there's a movie I want to watch with you. Have you seen Bird Box?"

Wrinkling his nose, Braxton shook his head. "I heard it was really bad."

"It's not Grammy worthy, but it's entertaining. And you haven't seen it, so it'll pass the time. You like so many different types of movies, but suspense seems to keep your attention more than anything." Ryan spoke as though him having noticed that was the most normal thing in the world, helping Braxton slide over so he could squeeze in next to him. "You can choose the next movie. Something unexpected you want me to give a chance."

"How about The General's Daughter?" Braxton ducked his head when Ryan blinked. "Umm...it's one of my mom's favorites. I used to reject older movies…" He snorted at the look Ryan gave him at the 'older'. "After I graduated high school and my parents were gone more, I wanted to share everything that interested them whenever they were around. I ended up finding some new favorites. Finally gave in and watched West Side Story with my dad, which made him really happy."

Expression softening, Ryan squeezed his hand. "Did you enjoy it?"

Nodding, Braxton sat up as much as he could, trying to adjust the pillows, then holding still when Ryan took over. He got comfortable. "Sometimes I hum the songs to myself when I'm working out. And my dance instructor was thrilled when I asked if I could learn some of the moves."

"You dance?" Ryan glanced over at him as he set up the iPad on its little stand holder. "I should've expected that after seeing you up on that stage, but not that kind of dancing."

"Mhm." Braxton smiled, resting his head against Ryan's shoulder. "When the team started working with the ice girls on figure skating, I wanted a bit of a leg up. So I added dancing to my training." He paused, a wave of shyness hitting him, but forced himself to ask the question on the tip of his tongue. "Would you...like to come watch sometime?"

Arm around him, Ryan didn't hesitate before he nodded. "I'd love to. I also want to start coming to some games. It'll save my TV from getting things thrown at it when I want to go after a guy for a dirty hit."

The mental image of Ryan getting all worked up while watching him play warmed Braxton's heart. The passion fans had for the game was always special, but this was different. Closer to home.

For the rest of the day, time both seemed to drag on and go too fast. The drag was because Braxton couldn't wait for the doctor to come say it was okay for Ryan to take his mask off. As much as having Ryan here made Braxton so damn happy, seeing the mask was a reminder of the potential danger. He wanted to beg Ryan to stay as much as he felt like he should tell him to go.

And the last was why every minute seemed to be eating away at their time together. There was no way this could last.

He was greedy, expecting more when he'd already been given so much.

But...

"What's that look?" Mask off from the second the doctor came in and told him it was okay, Ryan frowned at him. He approached the bed, cupping Braxton's cheek in his hand. "You didn't hold back with the doctor, did you? Your recovery won't go faster because you're trying to tough it out."

Braxton shook his head. "No, sir. I still feel like death warmed over and everything's sore. Not as bad as yesterday, though. And a lot of the symptoms they were worried about never happened. That old earache I kept getting isn't something I'm going to ignore anymore."

"Good." Ryan searched his gaze, concern in his eyes. "Then what is it?"

Sighing, Braxton stopped trying to look away. "I love having you with me all the time and it's selfish and I'm a jerk for even thinking about it. I'm just wishing we could have more of this. When I'm not sick. And before you say anything, I don't want this whole thing having scared you be what has you considering—"

Calloused fingers pressed to Braxton's lips as Ryan let out a soft laugh. "I already was. *Before* you got sick, so no, that's not what has me considering anything. I do want you close so I can take care of you. The idea of you being alone in your apartment? I can't handle that. I won't force you to come home with me if you're not ready for that, but I will insist you get someone to stay with you—or at least check on you regularly. I'd like to discuss you moving in with me at some point. When you're feeling better and—"

"Yes." Braxton grinned, taking some satisfaction in being the one to cut off Ryan this time, secretly hoping his Dom was racking up infractions he'd have to pay for later. "I want to go home with you while I recover. I want to talk about living together. I'll keep my apartment for a few months—it's more fair to my roommate anyway. But I want to do this. I can't think of anything I want more."

Exhaling slowly, Ryan leaned in to press a kiss to his fore-head. "There will be a lot more talking, but this is enough for now. I'll be honest, I feel a lot better knowing you'll be with me. I'm going to use up all the time off I have—don't argue with me, it's not your decision and I need to do this."

"I wouldn't dare argue with you, sir." Braxton accepted the glass of water Ryan handed him, taking a few sips before giving it back so his Dom could place it on the rolling tray now pushed over beside the bed. "Can I tell you how good I'm going to be to make sure you want to keep me?"

That got him a chuckle. "I plan to keep you either way, my boy. If you're ever naughty, I'll set you straight. If you're good, you'll be rewarded. No matter what, you'll be mine."

Whatever uncertainty remained faded to nothing at Ryan's words. Braxton stopped trying to force himself to stay awake, to hoard every moment like he'd miss it when it was gone. This wasn't something he was reaching for alone, not anymore.

Not for a while now.

It was something he and Ryan were building together. They'd already laid down the foundation.

And nothing had ever felt more solid in his life.

CHAPTER 18

"Don't you dare lift a finger." Ryan crossed the kitchen in the afternoon sun, biting back a smile at the way Braxton groaned. They'd been back for a week, and with Braxton's strength beginning to return his need to serve had him all too ready to push himself, too hard, too fast.

No way was Ryan having it. He'd seen Doms get lazy, accepting their sub's need to please and giving very little in return. A power exchange was only one part of a relationship. A deeply woven one, but not all about giving and following orders. Taking control needed to include taking care of the person who handed it over. Seeing to their needs.

And right now, Braxton needed a firm reminder that it was both Ryan's responsibility and pleasure to give him the time he needed for a full recovery. With constant checkups and meetings with the team doctors while they worked out the expected timeline for beginning physical therapy and his slow return to practicing with the team, Braxton was already doing plenty. But for a young man used to being on the move nonstop, it probably didn't seem like much.

Sitting on the edge of a chair, looking like it was a struggle to stay there, Braxton gave him what came very close to a pout. "Sir, these are my friends coming over. I don't want to make more work for you. Maybe this was a bad idea."

Brow lifted, Ryan held Braxton's gaze as he leaned over him, one hand braced on the table. "It was *my* idea, love. Are you saying your Dom was wrong?"

"No..." Braxton frowned. "But you've taught me enough that I would if you were."

"Good boy." Ryan gently patted Braxton's cheek. "One day, I'll have a few of my friends over and you can show me all those cooking skills YouTube has taught you. Tonight, I'll finish tidying up and then we're ordering pizza. Keeping things simple."

"Yes, sir." Braxton's head came up at a knock at the door. Standing too fast, he swayed a bit. "They're early, I—"

Shaking his head, Ryan lifted Braxton into his arms to carry him into the living room. He spoke loud enough for the men to hear him outside. "It's not locked, you can come in!"

The way Braxton's face reddened as his teammate came in just in time to see him being lowered to the sofa was too fucking cute. He ducked his head against Ryan's arm, and Ryan stayed close, giving him a moment to compose himself.

More perceptive than Ryan would've given him credit for, Scott immediately began the small talk. "This is a nice place you guys have here. Casey, baby, take off your shoes, you've been jumping in mud puddles."

"Sorry, Demmy." The little girl gazed up at her second...stepfather? A dimple showed under the dirt on her cheek as she began undoing the velcro on her little pink shoes. "Don't tell Daddy, he'll be sad that I ruined my new dress."

Scott made a dismissive sound. "No he won't, baby. He'll be happy you were having fun. I'll show you when we get home how easy it is to get the dirt off in the washing machine." Crouched down in front of the child, Scott glanced over at Ryan. "I hope you don't mind that I brought her? Becky had a meeting and Zach's been house hunting."

"Not at all." Ryan adjusted a blanket over Braxton, then went over to greet the three men and...the little lady. He grinned as he put the movie the situation brought to mind on the lists of the ones he wanted to watch with Braxton. When Casey held out her hand to shake his, he bent down to her level like Scott had. He didn't know much about kids, but it seemed reasonable not to tower over them when welcoming them into your home. "I hope you like pizza and soda? I also made brownies for dessert. Braxton's still building up his appetite, so I really don't want them to go to waste."

Giving him a serious look, Casey nodded. "You can count on me, Mister Detective."

"You can call me Ryan." Ryan motioned everyone into the living room. "Does anyone want some root beer? I'll call for the pizza now. I wasn't expecting you for another twenty minutes, so the timing's a bit off. Excuse the mess."

Luke gave him a dry look as everyone accepted the offer. He sat on one of the two armchairs, grunting when Casey jumped up onto his lap. "This place is practically spotless. Don't be all stiff and proper. We came as soon as we could because we wanted to see how Braxton's doing." His gaze met Braxton's. "That was a close one. I wish you'd told us you weren't feeling good sooner."

Moving his feet as Tyler sat on the sofa while giving him a concerned look, Braxton shook his head. "Honestly, I thought it was game nerves. Or maybe that I was catching a cold. It hit me hard out of nowhere. I promise, I'd've told you."

"From what I've read about meningitis, it's a good thing you got to the hospital so fast. The team doctor's have been keeping a close eye on everyone. Oriana sent her son to stay with Silver for a few days, she was so worried." Tyler rubbed his hands over his jean clad thighs, his brow furrowed. "It's not too soon for us to visit, is it?"

Braxton shook his head. "No, the doctor said I'm not contagious anymore—he's not sure I ever was, but they wanted to be careful." He eyed Casey, who'd taken over the remote and put a cartoon on Netflix, while apparently explaining the entire plot to Luke. "You can't be that worried, or you wouldn't have brought her?"

"No, and she's had all her vaccines. Oriana said some weren't as common when we were younger, which might be why you were vulnerable." Scott took the other armchair, closest to Braxton, then leaned forward to squeeze his shoulder. "I'm damn happy you pulled through, kid. But I know you. I get you'll worry about keeping your spot, but there's a bunch of dick rookies they keep sending up that no one wants around. You've got nothing to worry about. Take your time and make an awesome comeback next season."

For a second, Braxton's gaze went to Ryan. When he inclined his head, Braxton exhaled slowly. "That's the plan. I was given a choice to try to make it back sooner, but if I take the whole summer to get back in top shape, it's less likely I'll have setbacks. I want to have a long career and rushing things...yeah, definitely won't help."

"Good." Luke glanced over at Ryan as he came back from the kitchen once he'd ordered the pizza and gotten everyone's drinks. "Speaking of 'rushing things', you two are living together now? Word is you went and picked up most of Braxton's stuff from his place."

Protective, much?

It would be easy to get defensive, but Ryan wanted this for Braxton. People who cared enough to check up on him. To make sure he was being treated well. After avoiding Braxton for so long, Ryan had earned the wary scrutiny. Rather than push back against it, he'd welcome it. Earn the trust of the people who mattered in Braxton's life.

Ryan set the drinks on the coffee table, lips curving as Casey grabbed hers and Luke moved fast to keep her from spilling it all over both of them. "I did. Braxton is keeping his name on the lease for at least another three months so his options are open. But I want this to feel like home for him in every way possible, no matter how long he decides to stay."

"I'm not leaving." Braxton rested his head on the arm of the sofa, a smile tugging at his lips when Ryan lifted him up to put a thick cushion there. "I've been spoiled rotten."

"You should be. You're a great guy, Braxton." Tyler's expression softened as he looked between Ryan and his teammate. "Laura's always bragging about how awesome her brother is. I didn't see it until now."

Breathing became a bit easier after that. Ryan finally understood how the team was like one big family. He hoped to meet Braxton's parents one day, but until he did, *these* were the people he had to impress. And so far, he seemed to be off to a good start.

The movie Casey had put on drew everyone's attention while they waited for the pizza. Ryan lifted Braxton again to let his lap take the place of the cushion, enjoying the feeling of all the tension easing out of his boy as he lay against him.

When the doorbell rang, Casey leaped to her feet and ran over to answer. After carefully sliding out from under Braxton, Ryan joined her.

"That'll be fifty-seventy-five." The young delivery man, who'd been here before, held out his hand to Casey as Ryan took the pizza.

Casey's eyes went wide. "I don't have any money." She dug

into the pocket of her jeans and held out a few shiny rocks. "But these have to be worth something?"

Ryan crouched down beside her. "How about you keep those, because they do look valuable." He pulled out his wallet and handed her his credit card. The order was already paid for, but the delivery guy had made the whole thing into a game for Casey. Ryan was going to make sure she had fun with it.

With a serious nod, Casey considered the card, then handed it to the young man. "I'd like a receipt, please."

"Of course." The young man pretended to swipe the card in the reader, then printed out the receipt. "Sign here, please."

Tongue between her teeth, Casey scribbled her name, then handed Ryan his copy. "Thank you, and keep the change. Mommy says a twenty percent tip is good. You got thirty. I'm good at math."

Looking at the receipt, Ryan blinked. He'd added what he thought was a good amount, knowing it was more than expected, but not calculating anything. Smart kid, she was absolutely right.

The delivery guy gave a quick nod and grinned. "Thank you, miss. And enjoy your meal." He bobbed his head again. "Have a nice evening, sir."

In the kitchen a few minutes later, Ryan let Casey help him get plates and napkins for everyone. Children had never been on his radar, except when trying to comfort victims, but he couldn't help look at her and wonder what it would be like—a very long time from now—to raise a child with Braxton. He was so attentive and gentle and patient. He'd make an amazing father.

He wasn't the only one thinking that way by the bit of conversation he caught when he went into the living room with Casey.

Head buried under the cushion, Braxton let out a laugh cut

off with a groan. "I *know*. If I had ovaries, they'd be bursting. Or...ugh, that's bad to say, right? But...the *feels*!"

Practically choking on his rootbeer, Scott gave Ryan a look that said he knew he'd heard plenty, but would pretend otherwise. "Well done, tiny. Come sit in front of the coffee table to eat. Do you want me to cut it for you?"

"Yes, please, Demmy." Casey leaned against Scott's side as he sat next to her. "Kids at school think it's weird to cut up pizza, but I burn my lips otherwise and I don't like that."

"It's good to be firm about what you like or don't like, no matter what other people think." Scott gave a nod of thanks when Ryan got him a fork and knife. "I usually let mine sit for a bit to cool down, but with all the playing you did in the park, this will get the food in your belly faster and you need a refill."

Back with Braxton, Ryan helped him sit up, keeping the blanket around him. There were still times when he got the chills, but it was hard to tell how much of that was fear setting in. Yes, he'd been diagnosed quickly, and had the best care, but Ryan had been there when it hit Braxton how serious his condition had been. How many people didn't make it. Recovery wasn't only physical, it was mental, and Ryan was here for both.

Right now, his man seemed absolutely charmed by the little girls, his eyes bright with wonder, as though exploring brand new territory. If they were going to start setting long-term goals, Ryan had a feeling kids were going to be part of it.

And he didn't mind the idea at all.

His parents were going to love it.

"I want more soda." Tone changing from the sweet, enduring one to something more irritated, Casey left Luke and went to Scott, wrapping her arms around his shoulders and burying her head against his neck. "Uncle Luke won't give me any. It's *not* fair."

"You know mommy only lets you have two a day, and you

talked Tyler into giving you one at the park." Scott rubbed Casey's back. "You tired, pipsqueak? Maybe we should get going."

Casey shook her head without lifting it. "No, you gotta stay with Uncle Braxton. Can he be uncle now too?" She sniffled. "I'm really tired. Can I take a nap?"

Nodding, Scott cradled the little girl in his arms. He met Ryan's eyes. "I was hoping to talk to you more, but she still does better with naps. Some think she's too old for them, but her doctor says it's fine because it doesn't disrupt her sleep schedule at night and to let her set the pace." His cheek reddened. "Ah, yeah, so more than you needed to know, but I've been at parent-teacher meetings and heard Becky deal with all kinds of judgment."

"Becky is a strong advocate for her daughter from what Laura's told me. I respect that." Ryan motioned toward the hall. "You can bring her to our room to rest. It makes sense that all kids wouldn't develop the same way. She's old enough to say when she needs a nap. I can't see that as anything but good."

Shooting him a grateful look, Scott carried Casey to the bedroom, coming back a few minutes later as Ryan had taken over and fed Braxton the last few bites of his pizza.

A tender smile on his lips, Scott brushed his hand over Braxton's hair before he sat in the armchair again, helping himself to another slice of pizza. "You two look good together. We were prepared to issue some warnings, but I don't think that'll be necessary." Scott grinned at Ryan's brow raise, then winked at Braxton. "Looks like you're in good hands."

"The best." Braxton took a sip of rootbeer, giving Scott a curious look. "But what do you mean by warnings? Ryan's a cop, you wouldn't threaten him?"

Luke's lips slanted over the rim of his glass. "Not directly, no.

We'd just make sure it was understood that you either got treated well or we'd get creative. We're very good at that."

I'm not sure I want to know what that would mean. After having to save Raif's car from the antics of the 'Trouble Triplets', Ryan preferred not to have their ire aimed in his direction. He wouldn't use his position against them, no matter what mischief they caused in defending Braxton, but he'd rather stay in their good books because he was making their teammate, their friend, his lover, very happy.

Tone firm, Braxton held Luke's gaze. "Don't. I don't care what happens, I'm telling you now, I won't appreciate you getting involved. I can speak up for myself and if I ever have any issues, I'll deal with them." He huffed out a laugh. "If I ever get my ass beat for bratting out, though, I'll welcome your advice on recovery for my ass."

"That we can definitely do." Finishing off his slice of pizza, Tyler sat back against the corner at the other end of the sofa. "But you get all the free passes now." Concern shadowed his eyes as he looked Braxton over. "How are you, seriously? You look better than you did before the game last week, but Oriana said it's going to take a while before you're a hundred percent."

Arm around Braxton's shoulders, Ryan did his best to lend his boy as much strength and support as he could, knowing how hard the reality of all this was for him. He still had a long road before he could go back to doing what he loved.

But for the first time that the subject was brought up, Braxton was calm. Even managed a smile, though it was a little sad. "It will, but like I said, there's always next season. I love hockey, but it's taken up so much of my life, I've never gotten the chance to think about doing anything else. I'm gonna take this time for, like, self-discovery or something. Do some volunteer work when I'm up to it. Maybe take a few classes."

"You're a smart man, Braxton." Scott's encouragement

seemed to relax Braxton even more. "And hey, if you need any suggestions on places that need volunteers, don't be shy. I have a full list from when I was trying to redeem myself to the team."

"I'm going to take you up on that." Braxton settled into Ryan's side. "It was really cool of you guys to come over. And being able to be open about everything in front of you is...awesome. I can't even remember why I was so scared to own who I am, except...well, things with the league are still...you know."

All three men nodded their understanding. As open as the players were with one another, reality was, the sports world had a long way to go to be as accepting as it should be. Coming out could still be a risk for their careers and Braxton was more vulnerable than most.

He had a space where he could be himself. For now that would be enough. In the long run, Ryan couldn't be sure what would happen, but as he enjoyed some quiet conversation with his boy and the other men, it felt like at least one goal had been reached.

In this space, Braxton was safe and cared for. He didn't have to question his worth, wonder if his performance made him useful. There were no brand deals, no stats on the ice, nothing except him.

What he gave was his friendship. His truth.

And more than anything, there was a special kind of freedom to that. One Ryan would make sure he'd always have.

Knowing who he was…

Was more than enough.

CHAPTER 19

Sweat trailed down Braxton's spine as he ran up the incline, loving the burn in his muscles and the way his blood pumped, the rush of finally being able to push himself this hard again without his body begging him to slow down. Even with the air conditioner blasting cool air, the summer heat was merciless, but he didn't care. He was made for this.

And so much more.

"All right, Rocky, that's enough." Standing in the doorway, arms folded over his chest, Ryan chuckled. Already dressed in his leathers for their first trip to the local BDSM club tonight, he'd gone from being Braxton's handsome, loving Dom to a powerful Master with an edge that sent a shiver up Ryan's spine with his every command.

The way Ryan looked at him made it clear he intended to use that power in some wicked ways.

I can't fucking wait.

Grabbing a towel, Braxton wiped the sweat from his face even as he slowed the treadmill to a slower pace, then stopped.

He got off to cross the room, resisting the urge to steal a kiss because he didn't want to ruin his Dom's perfectly smooth black shirt—which had taken Braxton days to build up the confidence to take an iron to.

Look at me go.

Hand framing Braxton's jaw, Ryan stopped him before he could pass. "What's that little smile all about? Are you excited for tonight?"

"*Very.*" Braxton stared up at his Dom, not moving a muscle, settling into the security of his hold, his mind calm in a way it only ever was when Ryan claimed full control. "I was thinking about your shirt and how happy I was that I managed to iron it perfectly for you. And that I don't want to ruin it."

"Ah." Ryan chuckled when Braxton's gaze dipped helplessly to his lips when his Dom wet them with his tongue. "You did very well. But neither of us is making it through this night without getting a little...*messy.*"

A delicious shiver went over Braxton and he inhaled roughly. "I'm good with that."

"I bet you are." Ryan brushed a chaste kiss over his lips. "But let's try to make it to the club as presentable as possible. If you keep tempting me, I'll have to punish you, and we wouldn't want that, would we?"

Braxton quickly shook his head.

Which got him a nod, then a light patt on the ass once Ryan waved him on. "Go take your shower, then. Don't rush through it, I want every bit of you perfectly clean. You're lucky I waxed you yesterday or we'd have to delay your fun even more to get that done."

Cheeks heating, Braxton had a hard time keeping to the even pace Ryan expected him to walk around the house, his mind immediately going over the waxing and how painfully hard his confused dick had been by the end of the scene. Getting Ryan off with his mouth gave him the fulfillment he'd needed, but he was still really bad at not begging to find his release when Ryan toyed with him like that.

Thankfully, Ryan never kept him waiting for more than a day. Braxton couldn't help having a one track mind when he was that horny, which made it hard to do anything productive. Hard, not impossible, which Ryan proved by giving him small tasks and rewarding him by...making him even more turned on.

His Dom was evil.

And I fucking love it.

After scrubbing down from head to toe, in and out the way Ryan had taught him, Braxton dried off completely, then went to the bedroom to stand in 'wait position', still naked. The bedroom was kept warm for this very reason, though it didn't take much in the summer, just the central air not being on high.

On the bed, Ryan had already laid out Braxton's outfit for the night. Forgetting the position, Braxton trailed his fingertips over the leather straps, smiling up at his Dom as he came into the bedroom.

"That's what I like to see." Ryan returned the smile, coming up behind him, kissing his shoulder before landing a solid smack on his bare ass. "You happy, not you moving when you're supposed to be waiting. Let's try that again, pet."

Ass stinging, Braxton drew his shoulders back, squared his feet, and latched his hand to his wrist behind his back. He managed not to lean into Ryan when his Dom moved close to his side, cupping his cheek, then trailing his fingers down Braxton's chest.

"Much better." The warm approval in Ryan's tone was like another touch, one Braxton craved more than anything. Reaching out, Ryan picked up the straps. "Let's get you set up, I'm finding myself impatient to show you off."

The subtle reminder that Braxton would be in front of other

people like this—even some of his teammates, who were regulars at the club, which was owned by The Dartmouth Cobras upper management—sent a shiver up Braxton's spine. He wasn't shy, but this was different. Exposing a whole new side of himself.

But his focus would be on Ryan. On his Dom's pleasure. On each new experience.

Or...at least that was the plan.

Watching him with the intensity he always had when they were about to do a scene, Ryan tapped Braxton's arms, motioning for him to hold them up as he began pulling the straps over his chest, with a V right over the center. More straps were done up snug along his back, under his ribs and over his hips, until Ryan got to the ones that fit around the top of his thighs, framing his already very interested dick.

Next came the leather cock ring, or what Braxton liked to call absolute torture because having it put on was both erotic and a tease. He held his breath as Ryan secured it in place, heat spreading along his cheeks and down the back of his neck as he recalled the last time they'd used it. Braxton had playfully thrust into Ryan's hand and got his dick slapped in response.

Won't be doing that again...

Maybe.

The final part of the outfit was a pair of snug leather shorts and soft calf length boots. Once Braxton was dressed, he waited for permission to move.

Ryan snapped his fingers, giving the hand gesture for Braxton to kneel. Once he did, Ryan brushed his hand over Braxton's hair. "You're so fucking beautiful. I never forget how much I love you, but times like right now? It consumes me in a way I need time to truly absorb. I've played at sharing this part of my life with others, but with you I don't need to hold anything back. Because it's not mine. It's ours. You give it meaning and that's why I decided to do this while we're alone." He reached over, pulling a black square box a bit bigger than his hand from under one of their pillows.

Wetting his bottom lip with his tongue, Braxton kept his gaze locked on the box as Ryan opened it. Inside were two collars. He'd expected one, they'd discussed it over the past two weeks, but the silver one with the solid circle that would rest at the center of his throat was a surprise.

"I made sure it's long enough not to be too obvious when you wear it under your jersey. It's a day collar." Ryan seemed to study Braxton's face as he took the collar out of the box. "It's a symbol of my commitment to you, and yours to me, every hour of every day even when we're apart. You said you wanted a full time power exchange. I wasn't sure you were ready, but as usual, when you put your mind to something, you don't back down." He let out a soft laugh. "I love that about you too. Without that quality, I'd have missed out on the best thing that's ever happened to me."

Braxton grinned, waiting for a nod from Ryan that told him he had permission to speak. "I love it, sir. I love you. And I'm glad it's a good thing that I'm more stubborn than you are."

"Determined, my cheeky boy." Ryan opened the clasp on the collar, bringing it to Braxton's neck. "But this means I'll be even more dedicated to being with you, to your safety and happiness, than I was to keeping my distance. Because you've given me a precious gift and I'll never take that for granted."

The weight of the metal warmed in Ryan's hands settling against Braxton's skin sank him even deeper into the headspace of giving up control. His vision blurred as emotions swept over him and he cleared his throat, trying to blink them away. "Thank you, sir. So much. What you've given me means...more than I have words for. I've never been this happy. Never really known what it was like to have somewhere that I could be…" He bit his bottom lip. "Whole. Which sounds too much like 'you complete me' and that's super cheesy."

"Hey, it's a classic line for a reason." Eyes shining with amusement, Ryan took out the black leather collar, placing it around his neck a bit above the first. This one was tighter and thicker — not to the point that it would be hard to breathe, but he definitely wouldn't forget it was there. "Come, my love. I want you to see how stunning you look. Then we'll get going."

Rising to his feet, Braxton turned to face the mirror above the dresser, his breath catching at the sight. Next to Ryan, he looked...like he belonged to the man. It was the only way to explain it. The look was wicked, but that was what stood out most. The way they seemed to fit together perfectly, the statement of the outfits, combined with the almost protective stance Ryan had.

His Dom stroked his hands up and down Braxton's arms. "I'd like to bring you just like this, but if you're uncomfortable being seen in the car like this, let me know and I'll get you a T-shirt to cover up with. I'm bringing one in my toybag for the trip home."

"I'm good, sir." Braxton closed his arms as Ryan wrapped his arms around him. His Dom's muscular arms steadied him, and along with the leather, gave him the feeling of surrender on a whole different level. "Really good."

The car ride ended up being uneventful, no one even looking over long enough to give him that rush of knowing the straps made it clear *exactly* what he was getting up to with his man tonight. Only once they parked in back of the club, then went into the unobtrusive building did his pulse really begin to pick up. He'd felt a mild version of this when he'd filled out his membership papers with Braxton the week before, going over all the rules and safety procedures, but this was real.

I'm really fucking doing this.

With the man I love.

For all the world to see... Okay, maybe not all the world. No cameras allowed.

This wasn't a performance, it wasn't meant for anyone except the two of them. Having an audience here wasn't the same as when Braxton got out on the ice. It was simply having somewhere to go with people who'd accept them. No judgment. No expectations. Just an intense experience and the atmosphere to go with it.

With Ryan's hand on the back of his neck, Braxton took in the space with wide eyes, not sure how to process what he was seeing. A lot of the players were here—more than he'd even guessed were the least bit kinky, interacting with the queer ones openly. Sure, this wasn't out to the entire world, but it was out where it was safe and that meant...*everything*.

To one side of the main room, which had a dance floor, a bar, and a few pieces of bondage equipment at the far end, Sebastian Ramos had Jami straddling his lap, her hips moving in a slow grind, Luke on his knees behind her doing something really hot with his mouth. Scott was alternately grinding on the dance floor, first against Zach, then against Becky, Zach's wife.

The tour of the club was quick, Ryan exchanging a few brief words with several other members, humming his agreement when a Domme admired Braxton, though Braxton didn't fully catch what she'd said. His senses were overwhelmed, taking in everything around him, anticipation pushing away everything except Ryan's movements, his touch.

His Dom seemed to have expected as much, because he didn't try to get him to participate in any of the small talk.

Missing one familiar face after scanning the crowd, Braxton frowned. Then glanced back at Ryan.

"Go ahead, pet. Since this is your first time here, I want you to feel free to ask any questions you have, or voice any concerns, so long as you do so respectfully. Always address me, unless another Dom speaks to you first, but they'll ask my permission, so you don't need to worry about that." Leather bag slung over his shoulder, Ryan led him around the crowd that had gathered close to the bar. He spoke close to his ear, his hold on the back of Braxton's neck firm, but comforting.

Taking a deep breath, enjoying the subtle hints of lemon cleaner and leather, Braxton nodded. "I can do that, sir. And it's nothing big, I was just wondering where Tyler was."

"Ah." Ryan chuckled. "The rare times I've come here, I give my sister a heads up and she lets her Doms know so they can plan to come on a different night."

"But she didn't know you were gay?" The rumors alone must've made her at least suspect something?

Once they'd reached the back of the large club space, Ryan stopped them in front of a large, solid, frame-like structure. A tall man wearing assless chaps ran over, taking away the 'Reserved' sign and leaving a small folding tray off to the side with two bottles of water and a couple packages of Reese's Peanut Butter Cups.

Ryan stood Braxton in the center of the frame, facing away from him. "No, my boy, she didn't know. Unless invited to by all parties involved, nothing that happens here is discussed beyond these walls. Those who don't respect the rules lose their membership. That's how the club ensures the privacy of all its members."

"I really like that." Braxton's breath caught as he heard Ryan unzipping his bag. He held still as Ryan moved behind him again, undoing the zipper on his shorts and drawing them down for him to step out of. A familiar tap to his hip and he held out his arms, spreading his feet wide enough to keep himself stable, but give his Dom full access to his body.

Somehow, even though his dick and ass were exposed now, he didn't feel like he was on display for anyone who might glance over. Ryan's presence gave him the sense that they were in their own little bubble.

Leather cuffs were secured around his wrists and ankles, then chains were pulled away from the frame and clipped onto them, shortened so Braxton could feel the restraints.

Ryan ran his hand along Braxton's arms, then his thighs. "Comfortable, pet?"

"Yes, sir." Braxton steadied his breaths, making sure to let his Dom know in every way possible that he was ready. "And I remember my safeword."

Kissing his shoulder, Ryan let out a soft sound of approval. "That's my good boy. Now, let's see what kind of pretty marks we can leave on this gorgeous skin. I'm going to make you fly, my love. Then I'll push you even higher. If you're a good boy, I'll let you come when I fuck you."

If anything could get Braxton to be on his best behavior, that was it, though he wasn't sure how he could misbehave when he was restrained like this.

Or why he'd want to.

The floggers Ryan used were his favorite, black and red bull-hide he'd demonstrated the Florentine flogging style with for Braxton several times over the past few weeks after Braxton admitted how much he enjoyed watching him do it. He could picture Ryan now, taking off his shirt, muscles flexing as he began brushing the falls over Braxton's exposed skin in a steady rhythm.

From what Ryan had told him, Florentine flogging was very much for the visual pleasure, stroking a Doms ego with how many would admire the movements. It also became such a natural rhythm Ryan could focus on sending Braxton into the headspace he craved, taking his time to ease him in and make the scene last.

At first, the caress of the falls was like a massage, almost too light, but the pressure increased, heating up Braxton's skin. From his shoulders, down to his ass and thighs, each strike sounding out a bit louder with the impact.

Blood pulsed to his dick as the light sting became a flare along his nerves, sending his hips jutting forward, then back, his muscles clenching out of his control as he fought to keep still. A sweet haze filtered out every thought, leaving only the awareness of his Dom, the echo of some kind of music playing just for them, strumming different notes of pleasure that flowed from him to his Dom. He could hear it in Ryan's breath. Sense it in his touch when he paused to trail his fingers over the marks he'd left.

The flogging had stopped at some point, but Braxton was still riding the high, a bit apart from himself as the blaze ignited along his flesh kept burning, consuming him bit at a time in a way that made it seem like he wasn't quite solid anymore. Only when Ryan pressed against him, filling him in a slick glide, did he come down enough for a more carnal pleasure to join the boneless bliss that had taken over.

"There you are." Ryan's hand curved under his jaw, turning his head enough to claim a long, deep kiss that matched the steady thrust into his body. "Stay with me, my boy. I want you to feel everything I'm doing to you. Don't hold back."

Braxton couldn't if he tried, but nothing came fast. Ryan used the straps to pull Braxton to him, fucking him hard, then changing his pace until a desperate sound escaped Braxton's lips. He was so close, right on the edge, yet his Dom's finger was hovering over the trigger. Ryan knew his body, knew how to keep him here for as long as he wanted.

A bit of a mindfuck, telling Braxton he could take what he wanted so bad, then not giving it to him. All part of the erotic game they played. One Braxton didn't want to end.

One arm crossing Braxton's chest, fingers gripping the center of the straps, Ryan slammed in hard, then bit the side of his neck. The pulsing within sent him plummeting into a freefall where it wasn't just a release. He came apart even as he bucked in Ryan's hold, crying out until his throat was raw. His ass clenched around Ryan, drawing a soft curse, mixed with a laugh from his Dom, another wave of pleasure washing over Braxton as his Dom ground against him.

For a long time, Ryan kept him there, his quiet, soothing words bringing him down slowly. Braxton surprised himself with a whimper when the cuffs came off, for some reason sure they were the only things that kept him whole.

Then Ryan's arms were around him, lifting him. A bottle of water was held to Braxton's lips.

"Small sips. That's my good boy." Ryan thanked someone as a blanket covered Braxton. "Here, take a bit now."

"Mmm." Braxton bit into the chocolate Ryan fed him, shivering a little as he blinked away the tears he couldn't remember crying that blurred his vision. Ryan had brought him somewhere else. The music of the club was faint. His Dom was sitting in a big leather armchair, holding him. "I'm sorry, I don't know what happened."

"Don't be, you're perfect, my love. You did exactly what I asked you to." Ryan kissed away his tears, smiling down at him. "You held nothing back."

The pressure that had clung to Braxton for a long time had been easing away more and more while he'd been with Ryan, but it wasn't until this moment that he realized...it was gone. He didn't have to hide anymore, not with this man. Everything he was, everything he wanted, was bared to Ryan in every way.

Safe to share with him because of the connection between them.

A connection that had started with uncertainty, with so many challenges, but facing each one?

Made it into something that would last.

Something unbreakable.

ABOUT BIANCA SOMMERLAND

Tell you about me? Hmm, well, there's not much to say. I love hockey and cars and my kids…not in that order, of course! Lol! When I'm not writing—which isn't often—I'm usually watching a game or a car show while networking. Going out with my kids is my only downtime. I get to clear my head and forget everything.

As for when and why I first started writing, I guess I thought I'd get extra cookies if I was quiet for a while—that's how young I was. I used to bring my grandmother barely legible pages filled with tales of evil unicorns. She told me then that I would be a famous author.

I hope one day to prove her right.

For more of my work, please visit: www.Im-No-Angel.com

facebook.com/BSommerland
twitter.com/BSommerland
instagram.com/biancasommerland
amazon.com/Bianca-Sommerland
bookbub.com/authors/bianca-sommerland
goodreads.com/Bianca_Sommerland
youtube.com/biancasommerland

ALSO BY BIANCA SOMMERLAND

Sign up for my Newsletter for monthly prizes and teasers

The Dartmouth Cobras

Blind Pass

Game Misconduct

Defensive Zone

Breakaway

Offside

Delayed Penalty

Iron Cross

Goal Line

Line Brawl

Overtime

Off Ice Collection

Butterfly Style

Cocky Shot

Neutral Zone Trap

Tag Up

Winter's Wrath Series

Backlash

Diminished

Inversion

Off Beat

New Rules Trilogy

Polished

Gilded

Damasked

The Asylum Fight Club

Flawed Justice

Beyond Justice

Hard Justice

Cold Justice

Raw Justice

Dark Justice

Uneven Justice

Deserted Justice

Stolen Justice

The Asylum Fight Club Shorts

Out of the Ring

Double the Heat

Also

Deadly Captive

Collateral Damage

The End

Celestial Pets: Evil's Embrace

Forbidden Steps

Rosemary Entwined

The Trip

Untamed (Feral Bonds)

Solid Education

Street Smarts

Upper Class

www.ingramcontent.com/pod-product-compliance
Ingram Content Group UK Ltd.
Pitfield, Milton Keynes, MK11 3LW, UK
UKHW041825200726
13854UKWH00002BA/573

9 798201 683085